Map of Early Bethlehem

1 Community House
2 Chapel
3 Bell House
4 Brethren's House
5 Apothecary
6 Sisters' House
7 God's Acre

N

BOOKS BY RUTH NULTON MOORE

The Sara and Sam Series
  Mystery of the Missing Stallions
  Mystery of the Secret Code
  Mystery of the Lost Heirloom
  Mystery at Camp Ichthus
  Ghost Town Mystery

Other Upper Elementary/Junior High Books
  Christmas Surprise, The
  Danger in the Pines
  Ghost Bird Mystery, The
  In Search of Liberty
  Mystery at Indian Rocks
  Mystery of the Lost Treasure
  Peace Treaty
  Sorrel Horse, The
  Wilderness Journey

For Younger Readers
  Tomás and the Talking Birds
  Tomás y los Pájaros Parlantes (Spanish)

The Christmas Surprise

Ruth Nulton Moore
Illustrated by Allan Eitzen

HERALD PRESS
Scottdale, Pennsylvania
Kitchener, Ontario

Library of Congress Cataloging-in-Publication Data

Moore, Ruth Nulton.
    The Christmas surprise.

    Summary: In 1755, during the French and Indian War, Kate
Stewart, nursing a burning hatred for the Indians who killed her
parents and kidnapped her young brother, goes to live with the
Moravian community in Bethlehem, Pennsylvania, and is horrified
by their calm disregard of a threatened Indian raid as they prepare
for a special Christmas.
    [1. Moravians—Fiction.   2. United States—History—
French and Indian War, 1755-1763—Fiction.   3. Indians
of North America—Fiction.   4. Christian life—Fiction]
I. Eitzen, Allan, ill.   II. Title.
PZ7.M787Ch   1989   [Fic]   89-15213
ISBN 0-8361-3499-0 (alk. paper)

The paper used in this publication meets the minimum requirements of
American National Standard for Information Sciences—Permanence of
Paper for Printed Library Materials, ANSI Z39.48-1984.

THE CHRISTMAS SURPRISE
Copyright © 1989 by Herald Press, Scottdale, Pa. 15683
        Published simultaneously in Canada by Herald Press,
        Kitchener, Ont. N2G 4M5. All rights reserved.
Library of Congress Catalog Card Number: 89-15213
International Standard Book Number: 0-8361-3499-0
Printed in the United States of America
Design by Gwen M. Stamm

95 94 93 92 91 90 89 10 9 8 7 6 5 4 3 2 1

Not Jerusalem—lowly Bethlehem
'Twas that gave us Christ to save us;
Not Jerusalem.
Favored Bethlehem! honored is that name;
Thence came Jesus to release us;
Favored Bethlehem!

Old Moravian Epiphany hymn
written by Adam Drese

To our granddaughter,
Stephanie Rose Moore,
with love

Contents

The Dream

She saw them as she was coming out of the woods—
six dark shapes slipping through the trees like long
dark shadows in the forest just before the sun goes
down.

At the edge of the clearing they sprang to life, their
bloodcurdling cries mingling with the startled call of a
blue jay. She could see them plainly now, the feathers
in their scalp locks quivering, their scarred, painted
faces moving in contorted gestures. Brandishing tomahawks and long hunting knives, they ran across the
clearing to the cabin and pushed open the plank door.

For a moment there was utter silence—a stillness so
deep, as if the whole world were holding its breath.
Then from inside the cabin the silence was shattered by
one long piercing cry which ended in a quavering moan.

After that all was deadly quiet again except for the crackling of flames that began to flicker from the cabin windows like angry yellow tongues.

The dark shapes slithered from the burning cabin like snakes smoked out of a cave. They began to run around the clearing in a frenzied circle, all the time uttering their terrible cries. One by one they flung fire-brands into the log barn full of dry hay.

Their leader was the last one out of the cabin. He was tying a scalp lock to his belt thong. The hair on the scalp lock was long and chestnut-colored. With terror and shock she stared at it. Then panic swept over her and, half crazed with horror, she leaped from behind the bushes.

She was running across the blazing clearing when a hand reached out and caught her by the arm, pulling her away from the burning cabin. A door in the ground yawned open before her, and she felt strong arms forcing her into a dark pit. She let out a scream, but it was muffled as the door above her slammed shut.

It was her cry that shattered the dream. Mercifully the terrible nightmare slipped away, leaving her in silent darkness once more.

1

Kate and Johanna

Johanna Rau held her candle over the sleeping girl in the bed next to hers.

"Kate! Wake up, Kate!" she said, bending over and shaking the girl gently.

At the sound of the familiar voice, Kate Stewart's eyes flew wide open and she looked up into Johanna's troubled face. Usually those friendly hazel eyes were twinkling in a fun-loving way, but now they were serious and full of alarm.

"You have been having that nightmare again," Johanna whispered, leaning over Kate's bed and reaching out to touch her trembling hand. Seeing Kate's pale, frightened face and the blue smudges under her eyes, she added in a lighter voice, "But don't worry. It's over now and the morning bell is about to ring."

Kate blinked beyond the girl at the rows of narrow beds that filled the long garret room that was the Sisters' dormitory. Under the high arched ceiling candlelight threw long wavering shadows across the whitewashed walls. Small dormer windows showed gray in the early morning light.

As she turned her head to the windows, Kate discovered that her pillow was damp from perspiration. Whenever she had the terrible dream, she always broke out in a sweat, no matter how cold the dormitory was. Would the nightmares never end? she wondered, turning back exhausted on her pillow.

Outside, the bell on top of the Bell House rang five strokes. By the time the fifth stroke sounded, the Sisters and other girls were wide awake.

Katie tried to push the dream from her mind as she pulled on her plain gray dress, laced the bodice with its rose-colored ribbon, and tied the long white apron over her full skirt. She carefully tucked the snowy white kerchief around her throat and put on the plain white cap, called a *Haube*, that all the Moravian girls and Sisters wore.

When she was dressed, she fluffed up her feather tick, then joined the others who, two by two, marched down the stairs to morning prayers.

Kate studied the procession of Sisters on the stairs ahead of her. Dressed in plain brown or gray, they looked as if they had been cast from the same mold. Only the ribbons in their bodices and caps set them apart—the pink ribbons of the single Sisters, the blue of the married women, the white of the widows, and the rose-colored ribbons of the older girls.

When she had first come to the Moravian town of

Bethlehem, Kate had wondered why the Moravian women were called Sisters and the men were called Brothers. Johanna had told her simply, "Since God is the Father of everyone on earth and we are his children, that makes us all brothers and sisters."

Kate thought that was a nice way to think of everyone—as a brother or a sister. Only she could not imagine calling Indians brothers or sisters.

The chapel of the single Sisters was on the second floor of their big stone house. After reading from the Scriptures and the Daily Text, the Deaconess announced the work schedule for the day. "And with Christmas coming soon," she added, "we must get started on the Christmas surprise."

At the mention of the Christmas surprise, the Sisters and girls turned to one another with eager, shining eyes. The Christmas surprise must be something special, Kate thought as she watched the smiles on the faces around her. She wondered what it would be.

After the Deaconess dismissed them, the Sisters left the chapel, singing the morning hymn:

> Be with me, Lord, where 'er I go.
> Teach me what thou would'st have me do.
> Suggest what-e'er I think this day.
> Direct me in the narrow way.

Two by two the Sisters and girls moved down the stairs to the dining hall and kitchen below. When they were seated at the long table in the dining hall, Kate asked Johanna, "What is the Christmas surprise that everyone is so excited about?"

"Oh, Kate, it's wonderful!" Johanna's hazel eyes were sparkling. "It's a surprise for the children, and every year we try to make the *Krippe* more beautiful than ever."

"*Krippe?*" inquired Kate.

Johanna laughed. "I keep forgetting that you don't know about all our Moravian customs yet. You see, the *Krippe*, or Christmas crib, is the nativity scene, using beautifully carved wooden figures to tell the story of the Christ child's birth. There are figures of baby Jesus in a manger, Mary and Joseph, the three wise men, and angels and shepherds and lots and lots of woolly sheep. The entire Christmas crib is decorated with moss, evergreens, and red berries brought in from the woods. And for the children we print little verses that are hung on the evergreen boughs. All this is done in a room on the first floor of the Family House where the children live. The door to the room is locked and the windows are boarded up so that no child can peek inside. The Christmas crib is to be a surprise for the children on Christmas morning."

"It does sound wonderful," Kate joined in, sharing her friend's enthusiasm. "Can I help?"

"Of course," Johanna replied. "Everyone works on the Christmas crib. The Sisters and we older girls make the woolly sheep and print the verses for the children. The Brothers build the manger scene and carve wooden figures to replace those that have been damaged or lost. We needed more shepherds last year."

She paused to take a deep breath then hurried on. "The boys gather rocks for miniature hills and moss to cover them, and they bring in evergreen boughs from the woods. Then on Christmas day the door to the locked room is opened and the children rush in to see their surprise. Brother Joseph, the Bishop, always visits the Christmas crib and tells the children the story of the first Christmas."

"I wish we girls could help gather the moss and the evergreens," mused Kate, looking wistfully out the window at the bright November day. Across the lane the last of the russet oak leaves hung on the tall trees, and among them was the dark green of pines and hemlocks.

At home in the back country on a day like this, Kate would be out in the little orchard, gathering the last of the windfall apples, or in the woods searching for walnuts and hickory nuts. But when she had come to Bethlehem, the Deaconess had made it clear to her that no Moravian girl was allowed to wander off into the woods by herself. Sometimes Kate felt that the Sisters' House, with its gray stone walls, was a prison instead of the refuge Uncle Josh had told her about when he had brought her to Bethlehem a short time ago.

She was still thinking longingly of the bright blue day outside when the girls arrived at the spinning room for their hour's stint at the wheel.

Sister Magdalena, in charge of the spinning, frowned as her eyes swept Johanna's rumpled apron and the crooked rose-colored ribbon bow under her chin. The girl's gray dress and apron and *Haube* looked as if they had been thrown on her that morning. Johanna never tries very hard to look tidy, Kate thought, smiling to herself. But then Johanna was too busy enjoying life to be bothered with the Moravian virtue of neatness.

Before Sister Magdalena could comment on her appearance, Johanna slipped onto the bench behind one of the flax wheels that lined the room. Soon her busy fingers were twisting the yielding flax. Her mirth and laughter mingled with the hum of the droning wheels and the patter of treadles as they were worked by a row of nimble feet. Sister Magdalena's frown changed to an approving nod.

Kate and the other girls chose wheels, and the morning work began. Kate found spinning a dull, tedious task. Her mother had taught her to spin in their little cabin at Penn's Creek, but Kate had much preferred to be outside in the fields with her father and brother.

While they worked, the Sisters and girls sang the spinning hymns, accompanied by Sister Magdalena's zither. Kate joined in the singing. As Sister Magdalena had said, it made the work much easier.

> Know, ye Sisters, in this way
> Is your work a blessing,
> If for Jesus' sake you spin,
> Toiling without ceasing.
>
> Spin and weave, compelled by love,
> Sew and wash with fervor,
> And the Savior's grace and love
> Make you glad forever.

When their hour of spinning was over, Sister Magdalena motioned for the girls to follow her down the hall to a workroom where a group of women sat carding wool.

"You heard what the Deaconess said at morning prayers," Sister Magdalena said crisply. "It is our duty to help with the Christmas surprise for the children. Sister Esther informs me that we need more woolly sheep for the Christmas crib this year, and she thought you girls might like to make them."

"Oh, yes," the eager young voices exclaimed.

16

"Very well. Sister Esther will show you what to do."

Sister Esther gave each girl a bundle of fuzzy wool. Pulling some wool from her own bundle, she twisted it about her index finger until it was a tight round ball. With skillful fingers she molded a body out of the ball and a head. Soon it began to take the form of a woolly sheep. She stuck thin strips of wood into the body for legs and painted a vermilion nose on it.

When the sheep was finished, the girls were enchanted. With Sister Esther's gentle encouragement, they were soon making woolly sheep of their own, and the rest of the morning flew by.

After a dinner of broth, meat, and vegetables, Kate followed the other girls to the Bell House for lessons in the schoolroom. Kate had never gone to school before she came to Bethlehem. Her only schooling was her mother's teaching her to read from the family Bible, the only book they had in the cabin. Here classes in music, history, and literature opened a new world for her, and she learned quickly.

One subject troubled her, however. That day during penmanship her quill pen refused to perfect the ornamental lettering and her colored inks spattered all over her paper. She raised stricken eyes toward the tutoress, who told her to sit on a bench in front of the room until she could do better.

Kate took her place at the bench, her face burning with shame. She was relieved when vesper hour came at three o'clock, and she and Johanna could go to the room they shared with two other girls, Anna Catherine and Regina, for some free time.

Two by two the girls walked down the long hallway that led from the Bell House to the Sisters' House. As they were crossing the entrance hall of the Sister's House, Kate spied the empty water buckets standing by the door, waiting for a Sister or one of the girls to come by to fill them. Here was the chance she had been waiting for all day—the chance to get outdoors.

"Let's fill the buckets," she suggested to Johanna, who was walking beside her.

Johanna nodded eagerly, and Kate grasped one bucket and Johanna the other one. They were out of the building before Sister Magdalena could call out that they should walk and not run. "Grown girls and ladies never run," the stern sister maintained.

How good it was to be outside, free from the confines of the big stone buildings! Kate walked across the square to the longhandled pump by the wild locust trees.

"In the spring," Johanna said, "the trees are covered with fragrant white blossoms." Now they stood bare and gray in the yard that made up the Bell House Square.

"I'll pump first," Kate volunteered, "and you can fill the second bucket."

"I'm cold," Johanna said, hopping up and down by the pump. Her face lighted up with an idea. "Let's run around the buildings to keep warm. I'll run first while you pump. Then while I fill the second bucket, you can have a turn."

Kate liked the idea and reached for the pump handle. "Hurry up," she said, "so that I can have my turn."

Johanna started out on flying feet, her cape billowing out behind her like huge wings. Her long apron flapped around her waist and her white cap blew off her head and bounced up and down between her shoulders, towed by its rose-colored ribbon. Kate grinned as she watched her friend go. If Sister Magdalena could see her now!

Just then the bell in the tower on top of the Bell House sounded the quarter hour. As she pumped, Kate gazed up at the tower with its weather vane on top. The weather vane was shaped like a golden-fleeced lamb holding a banner that pointed to the four winds of heaven. Johanna had told her that the lamb holding the banner represented the Lamb of God, an old symbol of the Moravian church.

The Bell House at the back of the square formed the center of the block of large stone buildings. Connected to it and forming the western side of the Bell House Square was the new stone Chapel, where the entire congregation worshiped on Sunday and at evening *Singstunde*. In front of the Chapel was the five-storied log Community House, or the *Gemein Haus,* as the Moravians called it. Forming the opposite side of the square and joining the eastern end of the Bell House was the large Sisters' wing. Huge stone buttresses flanked the Chapel walls and those of the Sisters' House. Johanna had told her that these massive stone buildings were built like the fortress towns in Moravia and Saxony, the countries across the sea where the Moravians came from. Looking at them now, Kate thought how different they were from the small log houses she was used to seeing in the back country.

Before the first bucket of water was filled, Johanna came puffing and red-faced around the corner of the Community House.

"Your turn," she panted, her cheeks flushed with the cold. "Oh, that was fun, Kate, and I don't think anyone was looking out the windows to see me."

Kate finished filling her bucket and started out across the Bell House Square. To run free again and to feel the sharp November wind on her face was wonderful, she thought as she turned eastward around the Sisters' wing. She raced along the back of the Bell House and when she reached the Chapel, she paused to catch her breath. For a moment she lingered there.

From the Chapel she could look down the steep hill to the creek and the log bridge where the road led to Gnadenhuetten. To the north was the Blue Mountain and the Pennsylvania back country where her home had been.

It seemed a long time, not just a few weeks ago, when Uncle Josh had brought her along the Gnadenhuetten road to Bethlehem. But her life in the Moravian town did not begin then. No, thought Kate sadly, it really began with the dream—on a bright October afternoon.

Her thoughts went back to that day. . . .

2

Flames in the Clearing

It was the day she had stood in the cabin doorway and had looked longingly at the woods across the creek. The forest seemed to beckon her that pleasant October afternoon. Above the treetops the sky sparkled a bright blue, and the air was brisk with the smells of dry leaves and windfall apples. The right kind of day, she thought, to go to the walnut grove and gather nuts.

Kate closed her eyes and uttered a soft "Umm" as she thought about the walnuts in the nutcake she and Mama would bake for Uncle Josh. Her lips curved into a smile as she thought fondly about her uncle.

Joshua Stewart was an itinerant preacher. He wore buckskins and traveled the back trails to bring the gospel to settlements where there were no churches. Folks called him a circuit rider, and he and his big bay horse were a welcome sight in the back country. Not only did he hold church meetings in settlers' cabins but he brought news from the outside world. It was like a holiday to the settlers when Uncle Josh visited their lonely cabins. And it was like a holiday to his family when he came home again, Kate thought. His bed in the loft, where her brother Benjamin slept, was always ready for him. Any day now Uncle Josh would be returning from his circuit.

Kate turned and went back into the cabin. Mama was spinning the last of the flax. She looked up from her wheel and smiled at her daughter. That smile told Kate what a beautiful woman her mother must have been when their father had brought her to the settlement as a young bride so many long years ago.

But now Mama's face was mostly sober and work-worn. A pioneer woman's lot was sorrowful and hard in the back country. After birthing six children, Margaret Stewart had only Kate and Benjamin left. The other four children were buried in small graves in the grove of hemlocks beyond the cabin. From sunup until sundown Mama's life was full of worry and hard work. A smile on those thin lips was a rare thing indeed. Mama must be thinking of Uncle Josh's homecoming, too.

"I've a mind to go back to the walnut grove and gather up the nuts," Kate said. "Then we can bake the nutcake Uncle Josh is so fond of."

Her mother nodded and bent her head over the wheel again. "Might as well take Benjamin along to help you," she said. "That young 'un will enjoy a romp in the woods."

Kate took her linsey-woolsey shawl off a wall peg and threw it over her shoulders. She picked up two piggins, small wooden buckets, on the bench by the door and left the cabin to look for her little brother.

She found Benjamin in the barn, cleaning out the stable, a chore he never liked. Eager to join her, he put aside his wooden shovel and hurried across the barnyard after her.

They waved to Papa, who was chopping firewood in the woodlot in back of the barn. He waved back, then heaved his ax over his broad shoulders and split a log in two. They could hear the ring of his ax as they crossed the creek on stepping stones and entered the forest.

Their clearing was surrounded by thick woods. The little log house and barn, the garden, and the orchard reminded Kate of an island in the middle of a vast sea of trees. The nearest neighbors were from the settlement two miles up Penn's Creek. The settlement, which included their own clearing, was called Penn's Creek Settlement.

Benjamin soon tired of following her slow footsteps up the deer trace that led to the walnut grove. He ran ahead while she carried the buckets. Now and then he stopped along the trace to examine an interesting stone or a piece of wood. He liked to collect pretty stones and oddly shaped sticks of wood. He kept his collection on a shelf in the barn.

Kate looked fondly at her brother. He reminded her of a yearling deer as he capered about through the trees. Benjamin was seven years old, eight years younger than she. He had Papa's blond hair and bright blue eyes. Kate's hair was chestnut-colored, like Mama's, and she had Mama's gray eyes, too.

She called out to her little brother not to stray out of sight of the deer trace. He turned around with an impish grin that told her he could take care of himself. He is growing up, she thought. He was beginning to assert himself. Children grew up fast in the back country.

As they got deeper into the woods, the big pines shut out the sunlight and the forest grew cool and dim. Kate felt goose bumps on her arms and she called out again for Benjamin to stay on the trace.

Here, deep in the forest, the old fear came over her, the fear that had started that day back in July when Uncle Josh rode into the clearing with news of General Braddock's defeat at the Forks of the Ohio.

For over a year the French and Indian War had gone on in the west, with the French and Indians fighting the English for control of the land in the Ohio Valley. But the Ohio Valley was a long way off, and the settlers at Penn's Creek had not worried much about the war.

Now, however, with the English defeat, the French were encouraging their Indian allies to raid the English settlements throughout the Pennsylvania frontier, burning houses and massacring settlers.

Uncle Josh had stayed with them in July to help Papa with the first cutting of hay. Then he rode off again on his circuit, his saddlebags full of good food Mama and Kate had packed for him. Before he left, he had warned them to stay close to the clearing and be on the lookout for strange Indians. He promised that he would be back in October to help them get ready for winter.

All through the summer of 1755 the settlers at Penn's Creek were fearful and cautious. Nobody went deep into the forest alone, and the men took their muskets and fowling pieces with them when they went to the fields to work. But the summer passed peacefully, and no strange Indians were seen in the vicinity of the settlement.

"Most of the raiding's west of the Susquehanna River," an Indian trader, coming in from the west, had told them.

Now that summer had passed with no Indian trouble, the settlers of Penn's Creek forgot their fears and went about their business as usual. But the old fear still hung over Kate every time she was in the forest out of sight of the cabin.

She was glad when they were through the dark pines and had arrived at the walnut grove. She gave Benjamin one of the wooden buckets and played a little game with him to get him to keep his mind on gathering the nuts. "Let's see who can fill a piggin first."

Benjamin enjoyed the challenge and set about industriously, picking up the black-shelled walnuts as fast as he could and putting them into his wooden bucket. She let him win, and he was more than willing to help her fill her own piggin.

Together they walked back to the clearing, Kate's steps brisk and hurrying. But Benjamin was in no hurry to return to the chores that awaited him. He liked being in the woods and lagged behind. Kate was getting annoyed with his slowness, but every time she called him to hurry, he would fall farther behind.

"All right," she called over her shoulder, "you can find your own way home." And with that she walked briskly down the trace.

At her threat Benjamin forgot his boldness, as she knew he would. Running to catch up with her, he wailed, "Wait for me."

Kate smiled to herself as she waited in a sunny glade

for her brother. The sun was in the western sky now, but it felt warm on her cheeks as she turned her face up to it.

The air smelled of the forest, the rich loamy scent of leaf mold and pine. Kate drew in a deep breath then wriggled her nose and frowned. Mingled with the fragrance of the forest was a faint acrid scent—the smell of burning.

It was then that she saw the smoke. It was a billowing dark column, much wider than the line of smoke from a cabin chimney. It rose above the treetops in the direction of Penn's Creek Settlement.

Benjamin saw it, too. In a shrill, piping voice he said, "Look at the big fire, Kate! You reckon it's near here?"

"It looks as if it's coming from the settlement," Kate said, shading her eyes against the sun as she looked in the direction of the smoke. "Somebody must be burning a heap of brush."

"I want to see the fire!" cried Benjamin. "Come, let's ask Papa if we can see it."

As she stared at the dark column of smoke, she felt a sudden chill come over her, as if the sun had suddenly gone under a cloud. She looked away from the smoke and down at her brother. "It's too far away," she said sharply.

"Aw, it is not," protested Benjamin. "Let's run and tell Papa."

Now it was she who had to hurry down the trace to keep up with her brother. They could still hear the ring of their father's ax in the woodlot when they reached the creek and jumped across it on the big flat stones. They ran toward the clearing. At the edge of it Benjamin, in the lead, suddenly stopped and stared.

Then she saw them—six dark shapes slipping through the trees like long dark shadows in the forest just before the sun goes down. At the edge of the clearing they sprang to life, their bloodcurdling cries mingling with the startled call of a blue jay.

Kate grabbed her brother and pulled him back behind the bushes so that they would not be seen. She motioned frantically for him to be quiet. Through the leafy branches they watched the dark shapes make their way to the log house.

Kate could see them plainly now, the feathers in their scalp locks quivering, their scarred, painted faces moving in contorted gestures. Brandishing tomahawks and long hunting knives, they ran across the clearing to the cabin and pushed open the plank door.

Kate grabbed her brother and pulled him back behind the bushes.

"Injuns!" Benjamin hissed, sucking in his breath.

After he spoke there was utter silence—a stillness so deep, as if the whole world were holding its breath. Then from inside the cabin the silence was shattered by one long piercing cry which ended in a quavering moan. After that all was deadly quiet again except for the crackling of flames that began to flicker from the cabin windows like angry yellow tongues.

Benjamin dropped his piggin of nuts and let out a desperate cry.

"Mama!"

Kate put her hand over his mouth as they watched the dark shapes slither out of the burning cabin like snakes smoked out of a cave. They began to run around the clearing in a frenzied circle, all the time uttering their terrible cries. One by one they flung firebrands into the log barn full of dry hay.

Their leader was the last one out of the cabin. He was tying a scalp lock to his belt thong. The hair on the scalp lock was long and chestnut-colored. With terror and shock Kate stared at it.

Panic swept over her, and half-crazed with horror, she leaped from behind the bushes to find her mother. Benjamin followed close behind her, whimpering.

She was running across the blazing clearing when a hand reached out and caught her by the arm, pulling her away from the burning cabin. A door in the ground yawned open before her, and she felt strong arms forcing her and Benjamin into a dark pit.

She let out a scream, but it was muffled as the door above her slammed shut. Benjamin let out a scream, too, as he dropped down beside her on the cold clay floor.

3

Uncle Josh

Even though it was so dark she couldn't see, Kate knew that she and Benjamin were in the root cellar. She could smell the musty odor of carrots and potatoes mixed with the sweet scent of apples. And she knew that it was Papa who had lowered them into the dark pit so that the Indians wouldn't find them.

Standing close beside her, Benjamin was terrified. He kept screaming, "Mama! Papa!" at the top of his lungs until she grabbed him and put her hand over his mouth to stifle his cries.

"Stop it, Benjamin," she said sternly. "Do you want the Indians to hear you and find us here?"

But he was too frightened to listen. What he wanted now more than anything else were his mother and father. He pulled away from her and scrambled up the ladder that leaned against the side of the pit. He clawed his way to the top, sobbing, "I want Mama. I want Papa."

Kate groped about in the dark to pull him back, but the little boy was determined to get out. Before she could reach him, he pushed open the wooden plank that served as a door. Blinking in the sudden light, Kate reached up to grab him, but she was too late. Benjamin had scrambled out of the root cellar and was running across the clearing toward the burning cabin.

Kate climbed part way up the ladder and peered fearfully out over the edge of the opening. She watched her brother's quick, sturdy legs make their way across the clearing, his bright thatch of hair gleaming like a beacon in the slanting sun.

With her fists pressed hard against her mouth, she muffled a scream when she saw him trip and go sprawling to the ground. As quick as a hawk, one of the Indians swooped down on Benjamin and carried the screaming boy across the clearing and into the woods. It was the Indian with the scalp lock tied to his belt thong; only now, Kate noticed, he had two scalp locks, the long chestnut-colored one and the other short and fair-haired. As Kate stared with horror at the second scalp lock, she knew that somewhere in the burning inferno of the clearing Papa lay dead, too.

She felt suddenly faint and ducked back into the root cellar, pulling the door plank over the entrance. There was nothing she could do for her family now. Mama and Papa were dead and Benjamin was a captive of the Indians.

She crumbled to the ground floor with an agonized cry. She couldn't help herself. She screamed with all her breath. After that all feeling went out of her and she lay limp on the cold clay floor as if she, herself, were dead.

But she was not dead; she could feel her heart pounding against her chest. And alive, she knew that the only thing she could do was to remain here in the root cellar as Papa had wanted her to do.

She buried her head in her shawl to muffle her sobs and lay there shivering in the dark pit. After a long while, out of sheer exhaustion, she must have escaped into sleep because the next thing she knew she awoke with a start at the sound of a voice calling her name.

The voice sounded far away, as if in a dream. Her first hazy thought was that it was Papa calling. But when she moved stiffly on the hard ground floor and discovered that she was in the root cellar, the terrible realization of what had happened washed over her and she knew it could not be Papa.

The voice called again, louder this time. Kate lay fearfully listening. A moment later the door plank on top of the pit flew open, flooding the small cellar with bright morning sunlight. A man's head bent over the opening and a familiar voice cried, "Kate!"

With red swollen eyes she blinked up at the man. In a daze, she climbed out of the pit. For a moment she stood staring at him as if he were a stranger. Then, catching a sob in her throat, she flew into his open arms.

"Uncle Josh!"

"Thank God I found you alive!" Joshua Stewart's voice was husky as he folded his arms around her.

Like Papa he was a straw-haired, rangy man, dressed in the familiar buckskins that smelled of wood smoke. He wore a fringe-caped hunting jacket that reached halfway down his thighs over buckskin breeches. On his feet were stout shoepacs, patterned after Indian moccasins with leather soles and deerskin tops that tied well above his ankles. Tilted forward on his head was a wide-brimmed straw hat. He looked more like an Indian trader or a trapper than a preacher, but he dressed this way because it was easier traveling the rugged mountain trails in buckskins.

Uncle Josh filled his wooden canteen at the spring and held it to her dry lips. She drank eagerly, not realizing how thirsty she was. He filled it again and slung it over his shoulder as they made their way across the charred clearing.

The barn was burned to the ground, and the air smelled of bitter smoke and ash. Kate stopped and stared at the black, ugly remains of the cabin. Her uncle pointed to the little grove of hemlocks beyond it.

"I buried them over there by the other four graves," he told her. "I set up two stone slabs to mark their graves." He hesitated, then asked in a faltering voice, "Do you know what happened to Benjamin?"

She told her uncle that the Indians had taken him away. "Where will they take him?" she asked with quivering lips.

"From what I gathered from a survivor at the settlement, the Indians were Delawares and Shawnees. They probably took Benjamin to their villages in the Wyoming Valley, up along the eastern branch of the Susquehanna."

He looked in the direction he was describing and added in a grave tone, "The Delawares and Shawnees burned all the cabins in Penn's Creek Settlement. This clearing was the last one raided." He glanced back at the clearing with sad, troubled eyes. "When I heard rumors that the Indians in the Wyoming Valley were getting ready for the warpath, I came home as fast as I could. But even so, I didn't get here fast enough."

Kate looked at where the barn had stood. "They must have killed the chickens and driven off the cow and her calf with the horses," she said bitterly. "They took everything they could lay their hands on. There is nothing left to gather up and take along." She glanced down ruefully at her brown homespun dress and linsey shawl. All she owned was on her back.

Gently Uncle Josh led her away from the clearing that had been the only home Kate knew. She did not look back. She wanted to push the black, charred ruins out of her mind and remember the clearing as she had known it before the Indian raid.

Uncle Josh's big bay was tied to the shagbark hickory by the trail. Her uncle mounted and reached for her hand. She placed her foot atop his in the stirrup and he hoisted her up on the horse. She rode pillion behind him eastward down the trail. She did not know where they were going, nor did she much care. She was with Uncle Josh, and that was all that mattered now.

All day they traveled on mountain trails that the circuit rider knew well, having traveled them so often. The sunset was staining the sky with red and orange hues when they came to a settler's cabin in a cove in the side of a mountain. Uncle Josh said that he knew the settler and his wife and that they could spend the night here.

Kate studied the little cabin nestled deep in the cove. It appeared to be deserted, but Uncle Josh knew that it wasn't. Having heard about the Indian raid at Penn's Creek, the inhabitants had barricaded themselves in. When they recognized the circuit rider from behind a shuttered window, the settler threw back the heavy crossbar that bolted the door and made them welcome.

The settler's wife was glad to see Uncle Josh. "Can you bide with us a while?" she asked eagerly. "We'll send word to folks nearby and have us a meeting."

Uncle Josh smiled at her. "That would be fine, but I have a mission to perform first. On my way back, I'll stop for a longer time and we'll have that meeting."

After a meal of venison and corncakes, Uncle Josh took out his Bible and read to them from Psalm 91. The firelight from the hearth flickered across his long sober face as he read. His voice was deep and melodious. To Kate it rose like the echo of a waterfall and fell like the whispering wind in the pines. It wove a special spell for those who listened, and it made the ancient Hebrew verses come alive with meaning.

" 'I will say of the Lord, He is my refuge and my fortress: my God; in him will I trust.... Thou shalt not be afraid for the terror by night; nor for the arrow that flieth by day; nor for the pestilence that walketh in darkness; nor for the destruction that wasteth at noonday.' "

When Uncle Josh finished reading, the settler's wife leaned back on the settle, her anxious face relaxed and peaceful. "Amen," she murmured.

The words from Psalms gave comfort to them all, and even Kate slept soundly that night on a cornhusk mattress in the cabin loft.

They left the settler's cabin the next morning at first light. A cold gray mist hung over the cove, and the good wife hurried to build up the fire in the grate. When they were ready to leave, she put some corn dodger into Uncle Josh's saddlebag, along with a slab of homemade cheese. From the cabin door she and her husband waved until the trees and mist closed around them and the cabin was lost from view.

That day they rode through more mountain country, following the streams downward and keeping to the valleys. On they went, and on and on. At the end of the day, in a deep valley between two wooded slopes, they saw a cluster of log buildings.

"That is Gnadenhuetten, a Moravian mission village," Uncle Josh said. "We'll spend the night at the mission farm. The Brothers and Sisters will make us welcome."

As they rode along the Mahoning Creek toward the village, Uncle Josh told Kate, "The Moravian Brethren are a devout and peaceful people. Most of them have come from the countries of Moravia, Saxony, and England. They have come to America to worship in peace and to establish missions for the Indians. They already have several mission villages in the back country and this is one of them."

Kate stiffened at the mention of Indians. "You mean they have Indians living in their villages?"

"Yes, Kate, but they are converted Indians. They will not harm us. They are Christians and live by the Scriptures."

Kate's mouth flew open in startled protest. "How can Indians be Christians and live by the Scriptures and do to our family what those Delawares and Shawnees did?"

Uncle Josh shook his head sadly. "Not all the Delawares and Shawnees are warlike, Kate. The ones who live in the missions are as peaceful as the Moravians themselves."

Kate set her jaw hard and frowned. How could Uncle Josh feel this way about Indians—any Indians—after what the Delawares and Shawnees had done to the settlers at Penn's Creek? Indians killed settlers like her parents and ran off with little children like her brother. How could such Indians ever become peaceful Christians?

Hot tears stung her eyes. The sadness in her heart was turning to bitterness and it felt heavy inside her, like a sickness.

They rode on in silence, Uncle Josh shading his eyes against the slanting sun and Kate brooding over her bitter thoughts. They were approaching the mission farm when a stocky youth with flaxen hair stepped out of the mill with a sack of grist over his shoulder. Kate thought he must be about sixteen or seventeen years old. He welcomed them with a broad smile and led the way to a large log building that he called the dwelling house. While she waited for Uncle Josh's knock to be answered, Kate watched the boy disappear around the side of the house with his load.

A Brother, dressed like a farmer in a linsey-woolsey shirt and knee breeches, opened the door. He greeted them warmly and offered them shelter for the night.

"You are just in time to sup with us," he said as he ushered them into a room where a large table was loaded with more food than Kate had ever seen before.

The youth, who was called Joseph Sturgis, joined the others and sat at one end of the table with the men. From time to time he glanced curiously at Kate, but when she returned his look, he quickly bent his head over his wooden plate. There were no other young people at the table, and Kate wondered if he was the only boy in the village.

When the main part of the meal was finished, the Moravians scraped their plates clean and turned them over. A Sister from the kitchen appeared with dessert which was put on the backs of the plates.

"You must clean your plate well before I can put a piece of pie on it," the Sister told Kate, with a twinkle in her eye.

The meal started and ended with prayers and the singing of hymns. One of the Brethren, called Brother Joachim, opened his Bible and read from Proverbs. More hymns were sung until it was time for bed.

Uncle Josh remained at the table to tell the Brethren about the raid at Penn's Creek. While the men talked, the Sisters took Kate to the dormitory in the garret of the house where she was given a cot to sleep on. Weary after the long journey through the mountains, she fell asleep at once. It was in the middle of the night that the terrible dream began.

Her scream awoke her. Vaguely she was aware of someone bending over her and a gentle hand pulling the feather tick closer to her chin. Her mother, perhaps, she thought in her half-conscious state. Then she awoke completely and saw by candlelight that it was one of the Moravian Sisters.

"You poor child," the woman murmured, soothing Kate's damp forehead with her hand. "You are safe now. Go to sleep."

With a little moan, Kate fell asleep again, the tears from the dream still wet on her cheeks.

4

Bethlehem

Before Kate started out the next morning, Joseph
Sturgis gave her a pair of moccasins that he said
he had made from the hide of a deer he had shot.

Kate was grateful as she stepped out of her stiff,
high shoes and into the soft, warm moccasins. They
were made from one piece of leather with puckered toes
and long cuffs. Joseph showed her how to tie the cuffs
above her ankles so that the moccasins would fit, then
he walked with her to her uncle's horse.

He helped her mount the bay, and when Uncle Josh
reined the horse around, Joseph waved good-bye, his
flaxen hair shining in a shaft of sunlight that filtered
down through the trees.

They rode about half a mile along the creek to where
it flowed into a small river. At the fording place they

crossed the river to the new and larger mission on the eastern bank. Here, Uncle Josh explained, were the single dwelling houses of the Indian converts and a mission house where the leader of Gnadenhuetten, Martin Mack, lived.

Hearing of their arrival, Brother Martin came out of the mission house to see them off.

"Godspeed, friend," he said as he handed Uncle Josh a letter. "I heard of your mission to Bethlehem from Brother Martin Nitschmann from the mission farm. I have written this letter for you to give to Bishop Spangenberg when you arrive in Bethlehem. It explains your mission and the news of the raid at Penn's Creek."

Uncle Josh thanked Martin Mack and tucked the letter into his buckskin jacket. As they rode on through Gnadenhuetten, Kate glimpsed several Indians working in the fields. They wore no paint on their faces and looked quite peaceful, but she turned her head quickly away from the fields so that she could not see them. She didn't care if she never saw another Indian as long as she lived.

The trail out of Gnadenhuetten branched into two different directions. "The one to the north is the Warrior's Path to the Wyoming Valley," Uncle Josh told her. "The trail to the south along the river leads to Bethlehem."

"Where is Bethlehem?" Kate asked. "And why are we going there?"

Her uncle replied, "Bethlehem is another Moravian settlement on the other side of the Blue Mountain, Kate. It is not a mission village like Gnadenhuetten but the central church community where all the Moravian industries are located and where their Bishop lives. It is

39

a beautiful and peaceful town, and I have heard that the Brethren there will give a home to anyone who needs it. It will be a safe place for you to stay while I am riding my circuit."

At her uncle's words Kate drew in a quick breath. "But—but I thought I would be staying with you, Uncle Josh!"

The circuit rider shook his head. "No, Kate, I am afraid there will be more Indian raids in the back country this winter. No settlement north of the Blue Mountain is safe now. The only safe place I can think of to take you is to Bethlehem."

Kate was stunned at what her uncle was saying. Uncle Josh was the only family she had now. How could he leave her with strangers in a strange town?

The circuit rider continued, "With Martin Mack's letter to the Bishop, I am sure the Moravians will take you in. They even have a school for girls that you can attend."

"I don't have to go to school," Kate protested. "Mama taught me how to read from the Bible. She said there is no finer book than that."

" 'Tis true, Kate. But the Sisters in Bethlehem will teach you other things besides reading." Her uncle turned in the saddle. His eyes were sad and full of understanding. "I know how you feel, and I wish I had a safe cabin to take you to. When this Indian trouble is over, I would like to settle down in the back country and build a cabin of my own. Then I will have a home for both of us."

"Oh, Uncle Josh, couldn't we build our cabin now?" she cried, her lips quivering. "I can bake and scrub and spin—"

"You know we can't until the Indian trouble is over," Uncle Josh reminded her.

"Then can't you stay in Bethlehem, too?" she asked, fearful at what might happen to him if the back country was no longer safe from Indian raids.

Uncle Josh turned his eyes back to the trail. In a grim voice he replied, "There will be many lonely settlers who will need the comfort of the Scriptures this long winter, I fear. I must minister to them."

There was nothing more to say. As they rode along in silence, Kate leaned her cheek against her uncle's firm back and tried to keep the tears from stinging her eyes. How could she be away from Uncle Josh, living in a town among strangers and not knowing where he was or what was happening to him?

The trail to Bethlehem widened into a wagon road that followed the river through a pass in the Blue Mountain. On the south side of the mountain lay a wide valley of rolling hills. They had left the mountain country behind them.

Uncle Josh flapped the reins, and the big bay broke into a trot. Along the road wild asters still bloomed, their pretty faces matching the blue of the sky above. The ferns along the riverbank were burnished copper. A redbird flew up from a flaming maple and a fish leaped from the river in a silver arc. But Kate was unaware of the beauty of this autumn day. Every mile they went was taking her farther away from Uncle Josh and the back country.

The road to Bethlehem led down across the valley, and along the way they passed scattered settlements. Uncle Josh pointed to a line of low mountains at the southern end of the valley. "At the foot of those mountains flows the same river that we have been following. On this side of the river is Bethlehem. We will soon be there."

Before long they came to a large creek, which they crossed on a log bridge near where it emptied into the river. On the bottomland on the other side of the creek, they passed a big stone mill with its waterwheel and mill dam. On top of a steep rise was the town.

Kate gaped at the big stone buildings with their red-tiled roofs. They were larger and sturdier built than any buildings she had ever seen before. The one they were passing was five stories high. Little dormer windows protruded from the mansard roof, but the strangest thing of all was the long platform with a white balustrade around it that was built on the very top of the roof.

She was still staring up at the roof with its platform when Uncle Josh drew up the reins and asked a passerby where they could find Bishop Spangenberg. The man pointed to a building across the way and a little farther up the hill. "You will find Brother Joseph in the Community House," he said.

They rode up the lane until they came to a building built of square-hewn timbers. Uncle Josh dismounted and helped Kate down from the bay. He slipped the reins over a hitching bar and gave them a cinch. Then he led the way up a pair of steps to a little stoop. With pounding heart, Kate waited while Uncle Josh knocked on the door.

In a moment it was opened by a woman wearing a plain gray dress and a white cap. When Uncle Josh asked to see the Bishop, the woman disappeared into one of the front rooms. She soon returned with a portly, red-cheeked man who was dressed in a brown home-spun suit with a plain linen neckband around his throat.

"I am Brother Joseph," the Bishop said. "Come, we can talk in here."

He ushered Uncle Josh and Kate into the room and motioned for them to sit on a settle by the hearth. Uncle Josh introduced himself and Kate, then took Martin Mack's letter from inside his buckskin jacket and handed it to the Bishop. The Bishop turned to the window for light and read the message.

While he read it, Kate glanced around the strange room. It wasn't at all like the bare cabin rooms she was used to seeing. A colorful braided rug lay on the polished floorboards. In a corner rested a wooden sea chest with a black iron hasp and rope handles on each side. Next to it was a high-backed chair with a rush seat. Where the Bishop sat was a table stacked with many books and charts. The walls of squared logs and plaster even had pictures hanging on them. One was a portrait of the Bishop, the deep creases in his cheeks turned up in smile lines.

But now his pleasant face was troubled as he looked up from the letter. "I am grieved about the raid at Penn's Creek Settlement," he said, his voice tinged with a German accent. "I was hoping the Delawares and Shawnees of Wyoming would remain at peace with the settlers in the back country."

Kate stared at the Bishop with sober gray eyes. Maybe he would not invite her to stay, she hoped. Maybe there would be no room for her here.

But when the Bishop next spoke, he was addressing her. "We shall be happy to have you stay with us, my child. You should be safe here. We have always been at peace with our Delaware and Shawnee brothers."

Kate dropped her glance in dismay. Her throat felt dry and tight. As if from far away she heard her uncle speak. "You are in good hands here, Kate. Now I can go about my circuit in the back country with a light heart. And in the spring, God willing, I shall be back for you. I promise that, Katie. Perhaps then it will be safe for us to settle down and build our cabin."

At her uncle's words Kate's heart quickened and she even managed a brave smile. Uncle Josh had promised that he would return for her in the spring. The winter would be long, and she would miss him. But spring would be something to look forward to. Spring—and a cabin of their own.

"Come and see me off," Uncle Josh told her. "I have something in my saddlebag for you."

"Will you not stay the night with us?" the Bishop spoke up with surprise.

"Thank you for your hospitality, but I am anxious to get back to the settlements," Uncle Josh said.

Bishop Spangenberg glanced out the window at the cloud bank forming in the west. "But it may be a stormy night," he protested.

Uncle Josh smiled. "I am used to camping out in foul weather. I have a heavy cloak in my saddlebag to keep me warm and dry."

Kate and the Bishop followed him out to the hitching bar where the bay stood patiently waiting. Uncle Josh reached into his saddlebag and brought out a worn, leather-bound book. Kate's eyes widened with surprise when he held it out to her.

"Mama's Bible!" she cried. "But—but I thought it

was burned with everything else."

"Your father must have brought it out of the cabin when he saved your mother's body from the flames. I found it on the ground where they were both lying. I know they would have wanted you to have it."

Kate reached out a trembling hand and took the Bible. Uncle Josh took her other hand and squeezed it gently. "If you are ever lonely or frightened, Kate, remember the Twenty-seventh Psalm: 'The Lord is my light and my salvation; whom shall I fear? the Lord is the strength of my life; of whom shall I be afraid?' "

He bent over to kiss her good-bye, and for a long moment she pressed her forehead tight against his chest. He patted her shoulder, then turned to mount his horse. With Bishop Spangenberg by her side, she watched him ride off. It was as if all the world she had ever known were riding off with him.

Down the lane he walked his horse, but before he disappeared over the rise that led down to the bottomland and the road to Gnadenhuetten, he turned and waved. Clutching her mother's Bible close to her, she waved back. She kept waving even after he disappeared over the hill.

5

The Scar-faced Indian

Singing voices awakened Kate the next morning. She looked around wonderingly. The singing did not seem to be coming from within the Sisters' House where she had spent the night. The long garret room with its rows of neatly made beds was empty now. Kate wondered where everyone had gone.

The voices sounded nearer; they seemed to be coming from the lane outside the stone building. Kate leaped out of her narrow bed and went to one of the dormer windows. Looking down at the lane in front of the Sisters' House, she could see the singers. They were shepherds driving a flock of sheep up the lane. Coming after them were some boys carrying bundles of wood. They were singing, too.

What a strange thing to be doing, Kate thought. To

be singing hymns while leading sheep to pasture! No one in the back country did that.

When the singers and animals were out of sight, Kate went from window to window to see what she could of the town. Below was a square surrounded by the big stone buildings and the Community House. At the bottom of the lane was a larger square with a scattering of smaller houses and workshops around it. By craning her neck, she could see the top of the steep rise that led down to the creek and the road to Gnadenhuetten.

Kate's heart quickened as she turned in that direction. She thought about Uncle Josh and wondered where he was now. Along the trail leading through the mountains from Gnadenhuetten? Would he spend the night at a lonely settler's cabin in the back country? A wave of homesickness flooded over her. Spring, when Uncle Josh promised to return to Bethlehem, seemed years away.

Her thoughts were interrupted by footsteps clattering up the steep wooden stairs that led to the dormitory on the top floor. A moment later an eager voice called out, "Oh, you're up at last!"

Kate turned and saw a dark-haired girl, the same age as she, standing at the top of the steps. The girl's bodice wasn't laced properly and the rose-colored ribbon under her chin was untied. But her beaming, freckled face and fun-loving hazel eyes made you forget her untidiness. It was this friendly Moravian girl, with her merriment and carefree ways, who had made the girl from the back country feel less homesick her first night in the Sisters' House. The moment Kate had met Johanna Rau she knew they would be friends.

"Sister Magdalena sent me to see if you were awake," Johanna said. "You slept right through the morning bell. But the Deaconess said to let you sleep this first morning because you must be tired after your long journey."

While Kate slipped into her brown homespun dress and the moccasins Joseph Sturgis had given her, Johanna clattered on in her quick, breathless way. "Aren't you hungry? I'll take you to the dining hall. You missed chapel, but if you hurry you won't miss breakfast. And Sister Magdalena said that you may go with me on an errand to the fulling mill this morning."

After breakfast the girls threw their shawls around their shoulders and started out on the errand. After the rain last night, the morning was bright and frosty. They walked with quick steps across the Bell House Square and passed the Community House. Below, on the other side of the lane, loomed the big stone building with the mansard roof and the platform with the white balustrade around it. Kate stopped and looked up at the rooftop.

"Why is there a platform built on top of that roof?" she asked curously.

"That's the house where the single Brethren live," Johanna explained. "The platform on the roof is where the trombone choir plays chorales at dawn. They play them on top of the roof so that they will be heard all over town."

"I didn't hear them this morning," Kate remarked.

Johanna shook her head. "The Brethren don't play the chorales every day, only on church festival days, like Christmas and Easter. And they play chorales for funerals, too. It's an old Moravian custom."

"How do they get up on the platform?" Kate asked, puzzled.

"There are steps inside and a trap door that opens onto the roof," Johanna explained. "My cousin, Peter, told me. He and the older boys live in the Brethren's House.

In front of the Brethren's House was the large green square which they had to cross to reach the mill. Johanna called the square by its German name, *Der Platz*. But before they could cross the square, they had to wait for a string of cows to pass by. Like the shepherds, the herdboy was singing a hymn as he guided the cattle along.

"You Moravians sure do like to sing," Kate commented. "Early this morning I heard shepherds singing while they were leading a flock of sheep past the Sisters' House."

"Oh, we do like to sing," replied Johanna, her eyes twinkling. "Every day the music master from the Brethren's House gives us singing lessons at school. Everyone sings, even while working. It makes the work much easier when you are singing."

While they waited for the cows to pass by, Johanna went on to explain, "We have hymns for all occasions. We have cradle hymns, spinning hymns, traveling hymns for the missionaries, hymns for the farmers and shepherds. Our music master told us that the apostle Paul said, 'Be filled with the Spirit.... Singing and making melody in your heart to the Lord.' And that's what we do."

Kate noticed that each cow had a bell around its neck each bell had a different tone. As the big animals lumbered by, the bells sounded a melodious tune.

"Even our cows make music," Johanna said, laughing. She hummed a little tune herself as she led the way across the square.

They walked by the pottery and the forge, then followed the lane down the steep hill to the bottomland where they passed the springhouse and the butchery. Across the road from the butcher's stable stood the big stone gristmill. At the west end of it was the fulling mill with its own waterwheel and mill works.

"Sister Magdalena wants some cloth to make you a dress like mine," Johanna said.

Kate glanced down at her old, brown homespun. Her new go-to-meeting dress that Mama had made for her had been burned in the fire.

Johanna led the way inside the mill where the waterwheel powered beaters to shrink and clean the woolen cloth. They walked across the big mill floor to a room where the clothier and blue-dyer worked. The fuller, whom Johanna called Brother Popplewell, went to fetch the cloth. When he returned with it, the girls thanked him and left the noisy mill.

Before they started up the hill, Johanna paused and turned to Kate. With an adventurous gleam in her eyes, she said, "We're in no hurry to get back. Let's walk along the creek and gather some colored leaves. We can press them in our Bibles."

They followed the millrace to the dam, where they scuffed through the leaves along the dam bank. Most of them were thin yellow willow leaves, not pretty enough to keep. When Johanna spied a red maple on the other side of the creek, she motioned for Kate to follow her.

They crossed the creek on the log bridge and walked up the road that led to Gnadenhuetten. In a short time they came to a stone house that Kate remembered passing yesterday with Uncle Josh. It had reminded her then of an inn they had seen on the road to Bethlehem.

The house had a chimney at either end, and the front, facing the creek, had two doors and three windows. Behind it rose a wooded slope. In the dooryard stood the red maple, its dropped leaves spreading a crimson carpet on the ground beneath it.

When they came to the tree, Johanna stooped at once to gather the red leaves in her apron. But Kate walked around the tree to get a better look at the house. She wondered who lived here on the other side of the creek, away from the town. Was it really an inn of some kind?

She was about to turn to ask Johanna when she heard the door of the stone house open. She looked up, startled.

Crossing the threshold to the dooryard was a tall Indian, dressed in moccasins, fringed leggings, and a hunting shirt made of rabbit skins. Like a warrior, his face was scarred with horrible figures. Across his temple and down his right cheek coiled the image of a snake. On his left cheek two lances crossed. Across his nose and forehead was tattooed a line of round scalp marks.

Kate stood frozen, staring at the tall Indian, who looked just like the scar-faced Indians who had raided the settlement at Penn's Creek. For a moment she was too numb to move. But when the Indian took a step toward her, she turned on her heel and sped for the road.

"Indians!" she shouted a warning at Johanna as she flew past the girl. Screaming, she fled down the road and across the bridge. She would have kept running for her life if strong hands hadn't caught her by the arm and held her fast.

6

On the Brethren's Roof

The hands held her firmly until she stopped screaming. Then they relaxed and so did she. She looked around at who had been holding her and was surprised to see a tall, lanky youth, about the same age as the mission boy, Joseph Sturgis. This boy had light brown hair and blue eyes that were puzzled now as they stared down at her.

Johanna came running across the bridge. "Kate, what is the matter?" she called breathlessly.

The youth's serious face broke into a sudden smile. "I might have known my lively cousin would get you into some kind of mischief."

"It—it wasn't Johanna," Kate gasped. "It was that Indian I saw coming out of the house across the creek." She turned and ventured a glance across the stream, but the Indian was not there now. He must have gone back into the house.

"Brother Aaron?" Johanna squealed in a surprised voice. "You are scared of Brother Aaron?" She started to giggle. "Brother Aaron wouldn't harm a fly."

Kate shook her head. "It was an Indian I saw, not one of the Brethren. He had a scarred face like a warrior. Like the Indians who killed my parents and ran off with my brother Benjamin."

Johanna stopped giggling, and the boy's face turned sober once more. Stunned by her words, they stared at Kate, then at each other. Finally the boy found his voice and said, Brother Aaron has a scarred face because he was a warrior at one time, but now he is one of our Brethren. He is our faithful Indian scout and lives over there in the Indian House when he is in Bethlehem."

"And he can't get those horrible scars off his face," Johanna added. "But that doesn't bother us because he's so gentle and good. When you get to know him better, Kate, you will think so, too."

A scar-faced Indian—a warrior—gentle and good! Kate shuddered and looked away from the Indian House.

Johanna turned to the tall boy by her side. "Kate, this is my cousin, Peter. And Peter, this is my new friend, Kate, who is staying with us in Bethlehem this winter."

The boy looked at Kate with sympathetic eyes. "I—I am truly sorry about your parents and brother," he said haltingly. "Would it help if you told us about them?"

Kate sank down on the grass in the shade of a

54

willow. She felt weak and shaken after her encounter with the scar-faced Indian. Even so, maybe it would help if she told Johanna and Peter why she was so frightened. Maybe then they would understand why she felt the way she did about Indians.

The boy and girl sat down beside her. Kate drew in a long breath. It was hard to begin, but at last she told them everything that happened on that terrible day. She told how Benjamin and she had gone nut gathering; how they had seen the Delawares and Shawnees when they returned to the clearing; how the Indians had burned the cabin and barn, killed her parents, and had run off with her brother. Then she told how Uncle Josh had found her in the root cellar and had brought her here to Bethlehem.

When Kate finished, Johanna reached out and laid a comforting hand on her arm. Peter said gently, "You're safe here now, Kate. We Moravians are friends with the Indians, and they look upon us as brothers."

Kate looked down at her tightly clenched hands. In a low voice she said, "Who can be brothers to Indians who go around killing and scalping folks and running off with their children! I hate Indians. I wish they were all dead."

Shocked by Kate's outburst, the boy and girl were silent. Peter picked up a willow frond and looked down at it gravely. At last he said, "Hating and killing them won't make your parents live again, Kate. Brother Joseph said we must try to understand how the Indians feel. This was their land before the settlers came and took it, leaving them homeless and without food. Heaven knows how many of them died because of that. If the white man had treated the Indians fairly, things would have been different." He paused, then asked, "Have you ever heard of the Walking Purchase?"

Kate shook her head and looked away from Peter's sober eyes.

"Well, the Walking Purchase was made eighteen years ago, in 1737, by William Penn and his friends, the Delawares," Peter began. "William Penn was a Quaker and founder of the city of Philadelphia. He treated the Indians fairly, but he died before the Walking Purchase was put into effect.

"The men who came after Penn were greedy for land and interpreted and deed wrong. The land purchased from the Delawares was to begin at a point west of the Delaware River and run northward as far as a man could walk at a normal pace in a day and a half. That would be about thirty miles. But the white men hired three swift runners, who ran as fast as they could. Not only did they run fast but they ran inland, whereas the treaty said that the route taken was to be walked parallel to the river.

"Two of the runners ran until they were exhausted, but the third man continued on. When the 'walk' was over, the Delawares were cheated out of most of their land around here. They were driven from their homes and had to move northward beyond the Blue Mountain to the Wyoming Valley. Some migrated with the Shawnees farther west to the Ohio country, where they fell in with the French, who promised to restore their lands if they would wear the black paint of war and attack the English settlements."

"I know," Kate broke in. "Uncle Josh told us about General Braddock's defeat at Fort Duquesne and how the French were getting the Indians to attack the settlements. But back at Penn's Creek we never heard about such a thing as the Walking Purchase. All Papa wanted to do was to live in peace with his neighbors and the Indians."

Peter nodded. "That's what we Moravians want, too. To live in peace with everybody, no matter what the color of his skin or what his nationality is."

Johanna said thoughtfully, "What those white men did with the Walking Purchase was wrong, too."

Peter replied solemnly, "Yes, they were both wrong. Not all Indians have been told about Jesus' commandment to love one another, and not all white men have lived by that commandment."

Kate opened her mouth, then closed it again. What was there to say to this Moravian boy and girl who were determined to be friends with the Indians and to look upon them as brothers?

Johanna gathered up her leaves and the bundle of cloth from the fulling mill. "We better get back," she said. "Sister Magdalena will be wondering what took us so long."

Peter walked with them up the hill. The subject of Indians was dropped, and they talked of other things as they walked along.

After they said good-bye to Peter at the Brethren's House, Kate asked Johanna, "Why does Peter live in the Brethren's House and you in the Sisters' House? Why don't you live with your parents?"

"Peter's mother and father are missionaries at an Indian mission in the colony of New York," Johanna explained. "And my parents are missionaries on the island of St. Thomas in the West Indies, where they preach to the Negro slaves. We children of missionaries stay here in Bethlehem to be educated and taught a trade. The small children live in the nursery at the Family House, and we older girls and boys live at the Sisters' House and the Brethren's House."

Johanna went on wistfully, "I don't see my parents often, but I write to them every day in my journal, and they write to me in theirs. When one of the missionaries returns to Bethlehem from St. Thomas, he brings me their journal to read, and when he sets out for St. Thomas again, I send my journal with him for my parents to read. When I write in my journal every day, I feel close to my parents—as if I were actually talking to them."

As they walked across the Bell House Square, Kate let her thoughts wander. What strange customs these Moravians had, playing trombones on rooftops and loving the Indians and slaves so much that they lived apart from their families. Like her, Johanna had no mother and father to live with, and neither had Peter.

She thought about the tall, lanky boy she had just met. She thought about his young, serious face that could break into a sudden smile if it wanted to and the gentle blue eyes. Even though she and Peter did not agree about Indians, she liked him anyway and wondered when she would see him again.

It wasn't until a week later, the day the trombones trumpeted from the roof of the Brethren's House. Kate and Johanna were in the girls' room, doing needlework with Anna Catherine and Regina. Kate was so startled by the strange-sounding trombones that she pricked her finger with her needle.

Sucking her injured finger, she ran to the window and looked at the rooftop of the big stone building down

From the rooftop the trombone choir was playing chorales.

the lane. There on the platform were six Brethren playing long, strange-looking instruments. The tones were mellow and solemn, but loud enough to be heard all over town.

Kate turned inquiringly to Johanna. "I thought you said the trombone choir played only at dawn."

"They do when it is a festival day," Johanna answered, "but this is not a festival day. Today the trombone choir is playing chorales for Brother Leidick's funeral."

"He was called home yesterday," Regina spoke up. "He was very old—eighty years old. I heard Sister Magdalena speak of it at breakfast."

"The trombone choir will play three chorales from

the balcony, then they will march with the Brethren and Sisters to God's Acre," Anna Catherine explained.

Kate remembered seeing God's Acre, the burying ground, on the northern edge of town. It was a grassy clearing behind the orchard in back of the Bell House. The girls had pointed it out to her one day when they had gone with the Sisters to gather some late fall apples.

Johanna joined Kate by the window, and the two girls did their needlework together as they listened to the solemn chorales.

When the trombonists finished playing, Kate watched with fascination as the men left the roof. One by one they disappeared through the middle of it as if the big stone house were swallowing them up.

"It must be wonderful," she mused, "to stand up there so high and look down over the town."

Johanna's gaze followed Kate's to the rooftop. "Peter said you can see the entire valley, from one mountain range to the other, from up there." Her eyes were alight with a sudden idea. Lowering her voice, she said, "Peter knows how to get up on the roof. Let's ask him to take us!"

"But we have our needlework to do," Kate replied with a sigh. "Our samplers are only half finished."

"Oh, bother with the old samplers!" Johanna said, wrinkling her nose. "Now would be a good time to go. With most of the Sisters and Brethren at God's Acre, no one will miss us."

"What about Anna Catherine and Regina?" Kate asked, casting a sideways glance back at the two girls whose heads were bent industriously over their samplers.

"Oh, they won't go with us," Johanna said, "but they won't tell, either." When Kate still looked doubtful, she added with an impish grin, "It's not as if we would be committing a sin!"

Kate grinned back and ran her needle several times into the cloth to hold it. "All right. Let's go!"

Quickly they laid their samplers on the table. Before Anna Catherine or Regina could ask where they were going, they slipped out of the room. They were relieved to see that the hall and stairway were empty, and no one saw them as they hurried down the stairs.

They waited until the trombonists had passed solemnly out of the front door of the Brethren's House before they crossed the Bell House Square and hurried down the lane. When they came to the big stone house, Johanna looked around furtively to see if anyone was watching, then whispered, "Follow me inside and don't make a sound."

They entered a narrow hall on the first floor that led past the workrooms of the Brothers. In one room Kate glimpsed a weaver's big loom. In another room she heard the tack-tack-tack of a shoemaker's small hammer. Except for the shoemaker, it seemed that all the workers had gone to the burying ground.

Johanna led the way to a room at the back of the building that had the smell of new leather about it. She motioned Kate to her side and whispered, "Peter works here in the saddlery. I hope he's here and alone."

They were in luck. Peter was there and he was alone. He was dressed in a long leather apron, the sleeves of his homespun shirt rolled up. He was polishing a new saddle on a saddle rack. He looked up with surprise when he saw the two girls standing in the doorway.

"What are you doing here?" he said in a hushed voice so that the shoemaker wouldn't hear. "You know no girls are allowed in the Brethren's House." He frowned at the eager look on his cousin's face, at her wide, excited eyes. Knowing that look, he knew she was up to something.

"Oh, Peter, we want to go up to the roof to see the view from the platform. Please take us."

The tall youth was almost beside himself. "To the roof!" he breathed in a sharp whisper. "Johanna, you know nobody is allowed up there except the trombone choir."

"You were up once," she challenged.

"But I'm a boy and I live here."

Johanna stuck out her jaw firmly. "Well, we're girls and live at the Sisters' House, but we want to go up anyway."

"Johanna, are you daft?"

With a toss of her head, Johanna was more persistent than ever. "If you won't take us, Peter, we'll go ourselves. Come on, Kate."

Kate was torn between the two cousins. She would have been willing to listen to Peter, although she did not see why she and Johanna couldn't go up to the roof platform just because they were girls and didn't live in the Brethren's House.

Peter threw his polishing cloth over the saddle and shook his head. He knew how determined his cousin could be. "Oh, come along," he finally gave in. "It'll be quicker to get you out of here if I show you the way."

"Most everyone is at God's Acre," Kate said encouragingly, "so it's a good time to go."

Peter shushed her and listened for the rhythmic

tack-tack-tack of the shoemaker's hammer. Then he waved them on to a dim, narrow staircase in the center of the building. Before climbing the steps, he turned to them with his finger across his lips for silence.

They nodded solemnly and followed after him, feeling their way up each dark step. Stealthily they climbed the four steep flights. At the top of a narrow upper staircase, Peter stopped and felt around for the rope which opened the trapdoor in the roof. After he had raised it, he climbed out upon the platform and pulled both girls after him into the wind.

Kate looked out over the white balustrade and caught her breath.

"Oh, isn't this wonderful!" squealed Johanna.

From where they stood they could look over the entire town of Bethlehem with its stone buildings and red-tile roofs. Beyond the Bell House was the gathering of Brothers and Sisters standing together in God's Acre. They could even hear the distant strains of the hymns the congregation was singing, accompanied by the trombones.

Peter pointed out the large barn and other farm buildings clustered together at the northern edge of town and the fields and pastures in the wide valley beyond. He is right, Kate thought. You can see the entire valley and the two mountain ranges from here. She gazed at the Blue Mountain that stretched as straight as a line along the northern horizon. "The mountain does look blue from a distance," she exclaimed.

They turned to the south where a group of smaller mountains formed the southern end of the valley. At the foot of the mountain directly across from them sparkled the river with its picturesque islands.

"That long island in the river below us is called Sand Island," Johanna explained. Kate noticed a flock of sheep grazing at the eastern end of the island.

"And over there is the Crown Inn," Peter said, pointing to a large log building on the opposite shore of the river with a cluster of outbuildings around it. "The road to the east of it, that turns south around the shoulder of the mountain, is the road to Philadelphia, some fifty miles away."

"Travelers coming to Bethlehem stay at the inn," Johanna added. "The ferry landing is there and a flatboat to bring them across the river."

The river with its island is beautiful, Kate thought. But she turned once more to look at the Blue Mountain. The scene before her blurred as she thought about the clearing and the cabin beyond that mountain. A pain spread through her, a pain of wanting to be there but knowing that she never could go back to that cabin again.

Peter's urgent voice broke through her sad thoughts. "We better leave now. Be quiet on the way down so that the shoemaker won't hear us."

He helped the girls through the opening in the roof, then closed the trapdoor. Down the dark stairs they crept, Peter leading the way.

He was about to sigh a breath of relief that they were almost down the last flight when Kate's foot missed the next step. Before she could grab the railing to stop herself, she fell against Johanna in front of her. Johanna lost her balance and fell against Peter. The three of them tumbled down the remaining steps together and landed with a loud thump on the floor below.

The girls forgot themselves and screamed. This brought the shoemaker hurrying from his workroom to see what all the commotion was. He helped them to their feet and they brushed themselves off.

"Are you all right?" the shoemaker asked them.

They felt their arms and legs. Except for bruises, they thought they were all right. They nodded mutely.

When he was certain that no bones had been broken, the shoemaker gave the three of them a disapproving look and returned to his workroom.

Peter told the girls in a husky, choked voice, "You better go now."

He was red in the face, and Kate couldn't tell whether it was from anger with them for having talked him into taking them up on the roof or from the shame he felt that the shoemaker had found the three of them sprawled on the floor of the Brethren's House.

7

Disturbing News

The next day a stern Sister Magdalena told Kate and Johanna that the Deaconess wanted to see them in her rooms. Sister Magdalena did not tell the girls why the Deaconess had sent for them, but they guessed it had something to do with their adventure in the Brethren's House. The shoemaker must have told the Sisters about finding them there.

With dragging footsteps the girls made their way down the hallway of the second floor. Johanna gave a gentle rap on the door at the end of the hall, and a voice called out for them to enter. Johanna opened the door that led into a private apartment of two rooms, with its own small entrance hall.

The Deaconess was an older woman who was in charge of the Sisters' House. Her face was pale and lined, and she looked quite frail. But she sat straight in her chair, and her china-blue eyes snapped as she looked at the two anxious girls standing before her.

She came to the point of their visit at once. Addressing Johanna, she said, "You know that nobody is allowed on the Brethren's roof except the trombone choir."

Johanna nodded and hung her head. She kept twisting the ribbon on her cap until it was as limp as a piece of cord. She looked more disheveled than ever under the Deaconess' disapproving eye.

Feeling sorry for her friend, Kate burst out, "But we didn't mean to do anything wrong. We just wanted to see the view from the top of the roof."

Taken aback by Kate's outburst, the Deaconess rapped her knuckles on the arm of her chair for silence. Kate withered before the reproachful eyes fixed upon her.

"Girls are not allowed inside the Brethren's House," the Deaconess said. "I believe Sister Magdalena made that quite clear to you the day you arrived here." She leaned forward in her chair, as if to examine Kate closely. "We want you to be happy here, Catherine, but you must obey the rules as our Moravian girls do."

Kate cringed. Her parents had never called her by her given name unless they were scolding her.

The Deaconess sat erect on the edge of her chair. "You must both be punished, I fear," she pronounced. "For two weeks you are not to leave the Sisters' House unless you are sent on an errand, and vesper hour will be taken away from you. Johanna, you will be confined to the spinning room under the guidance of Sister Magdalena. And you, Catherine, will be confined to the kitchen, where you will help Sister Sophia. Now you may leave."

Subdued, the girls walked slowly down the hall. Kate asked in a tight voice, "Does that mean we can't be together for two whole weeks?"

Johanna nodded, but there was still some sparkle left in her hazel eyes. "We can see each other every night at bedtime, though, and then we can talk and tell each other everything we did that day."

That was some consolation, Kate thought with a sigh. After leaving Johanna at the spinning room, Kate made her way down to the kitchen. She felt very much alone without Johanna walking beside her. Since Kate had been in Bethlehem, Johanna had been her constant companion. The days would be long without Johanna's sparkling laughter to keep him from being homesick.

Sister Sophia was busy straining apples for sauce when Kate arrived at the kitchen. She was singing a hymn in German while she worked, but stopped when she saw the girl.

Sister Sophia was a large woman with a round, shiny face. Her curly red hair, now faded to a sandy hue, escaped in stray ringlets from the confines of her cap. Her *Haube* was tied around her chin with the white widow's bow.

With a wry smile she greeted Kate by saying, "So you are being punished because you went up to the Brethren's roof, eh? Well, girls will be girls, as they say. I'm just happy to have a girl for a while to help me with my chores. What can you do?"

Relieved at not getting another scolding, Kate answered eagerly, "I can bake. I baked most of the bread at home, and Mama said I was good at it."

"Well, now, that's fine," Sister Sophia said, beaming. "We have white flour, rye, and Indian maize, fresh from the mill." She left her straining and bustled off for the flour.

While she waited for the cook to return, Kate's glance took in the big kitchen. From thick ceiling beams hung bunches of herbs to dry. In the middle of the room stood a large worktable. The far wall was taken up by a great fireplace. From an iron crane, swung over the burning logs, a kettle of apples bubbled, filling the kitchen with their spicy aroma.

When Sister Sophia returned with the flour, Kate rolled up her sleeves and got to work. Soon she was kneading the dough for the bread, her hands and arms white with flour. She made a dozen loaves of bread that day, as much as the two side ovens built into the fireplace walls could hold. When the golden brown loaves were baked, the cook praised her.

That night before the girls went to sleep, they whispered together in the garret dormitory. From what Johanna told Kate about her long day's work at the spinning wheel, Kate was relieved that it was Sister Sophia she had been assigned to. Poor Johanna under Sister Magdalena's stern eye!

But when Johanna started imitating Sister Magdalena's bossy commands in a high, shrill whisper, they both fell into such fits of giggling that a loud "Sssh" sounded from a Sister's bed nearby.

At once the girls stopped whispering and stifled their giggles in their pillows. Johanna soon dropped off to sleep, and Kate rolled over on her narrow bed to listen for the watchman. In a short while he came, chanting a little rhyme as he called the hour.

'Tis nine o'clock! Ye Brethren, hear it striking;
Keep hearts and houses clean to our Savior's liking.

Kate wondered how poor Peter was being punished. It was really her and Johanna's fault that he got into trouble. She sighed and wondered if he would ever forgive them. But before she could worry any more about it, she, too, was sound asleep and did not hear the watchman sing out:

Now, Brethren, hear! The clock is ten and passing. . . .

The next morning when Kate hurried down to the kitchen to help Sister Sophia prepare breakfast, she was surprised to find one of the Brethren sitting at the kitchen table. His two red hands were wrapped around a mug of steaming hot coffee. Sister Sophia was hovering over him with a pan of freshly baked biscuits.

"Have a biscuit, Brother Matthias," she said, placing a piping hot biscuit on his plate.

The man swallowed some coffee, then unwound his muffler and unbottoned his heavy greatcoat. His cheeks bulged as he popped half the biscuit into his mouth. He was a big man with sandy eyebrows and friendly blue eyes.

"This is Brother Matthias, our watchman," Sister Sophia told Kate, smiling down at the man. "He stops in now and then for a cup of coffee before going off duty."

"And to tell you all the latest news," Brother Matthias reminded her with a chuckle.

"Well, and that, too," Sister Sophia admitted, her white bow bobbing up and down beneath her plump chin.

Curiously Kate asked, "Why do you call out the nours by singing rhymes, Brother Matthias?"

The jovial watchman leaned back in his chair and smiled. "Ach, a bit of singing is like a mother crooning her babe to sleep. It settles one down after a long, hard day."

"And Brother Matthias does have such a lovely baritone," added Sister Sophia, beaming another smile at the watchman.

After a second cup of coffee, Brother Matthias arose stiffly from the table. "I must get to my bed before I fall asleep in this warm, cozy kitchen." He buttoned his long greatcoat and wound the muffler around his neck. "A bit of frost last night," he said. "It won't be long before the snow flies."

He picked up his handmade iron lantern, but before he opened the door to leave, he turned to Sister Sophia. "Last night two missionaries returned to Bethlehem," he said. "Brother David Zeisberger and Brother Christian Seidel."

"Is that so?" replied the cook, pausing over another pan of biscuits she was drawing from the oven.

Brother Matthias nodded. "When I met them, they spoke briefly of their return to Bethlehem. They had been at the Wyoming Valley, where they were trying to persuade our Indian deserters against joining the French. But the French Indians are in an ugly mood, they said, and our Moravian Indians are too frightened to return to our missions. When Brother David's and Brother Christian's own lives were threatened, they had to leave the Wyoming Valley and return to Bethlehem. They are at the Community House now, reporting to Brother Joseph and the elders."

Sister Sophia threw her big apron up over her face in a gesture of despair. "I am glad they are safe," she cried, "but what distressing news they bring back with them."

"Ach, mark my words, Sister, there will be raiding in the back country this winter," Brother Matthias predicted solemnly. With that he pulled on his hat and clumped out of the kitchen. The sound of feet approaching the dining room sent Kate and Sister Sophia scurrying around the kitchen to prepare breakfast. For the next hour they were so busy with bowls of mush, plates of biscuits, and mugs of hot coffee that they had no time to think about Brother Matthias' disturbing news.

Later, when they were having their own breakfast at the kitchen table, Kate asked the cook, "Why does Brother Matthias and everyone in Bethlehem call the Bishop by the name of Brother Joseph? Is that his given name?"

"No," replied Sister Sophia, "his name is Augustus Gottlieb Spangenberg. Count Zinzendorf, our benefactor from Saxony, gave him the name Brother Joseph because, like Joseph in the Bible, he takes good care of his brothers." Sister Sophia smiled affectionately. "We all love and respect Brother Joseph. He is our spiritual leader and truly a brother to us all."

Kate thought about the portly, red-cheeked man dressed in the plain brown suit. She remembered how caring he had been when she had first met him and how he had welcomed her to Bethlehem. "We shall be happy to have you stay with us, my child," he had told her. "You should be safe here. We have always been at peace with our Delaware and Shawnee brothers."

But now two Moravian missionaries, fearing for

their lives, had fled from the Wyoming Valley. What would Brother Joseph be thinking today when he heard their news? Would the peace between the Moravians and the Delawares and Shawnees be broken? Would Brother Matthias' prediction come true? Kate felt the familiar ache of fear return to her.

A thump outside the kitchen door brought her out of her troubled thoughts.

" 'Tis the boy with the firewood," Sister Sophia said. "Go out and fetch some sticks for the fire, Kate."

Kate threw on the warm woolen cloak the Sisters had made for her and stepped out the kitchen door. A tall boy was bent over, unloading wood from a heavy burlap sack. When he had filled the woodbox, he straightened and turned to her.

Both stared at each other with surprise. Then both of them exclaimed at the same time, "Peter!" "Kate!"

8

The Christmas Story

Peter gave Kate a broad grin. She was so relieved that he wasn't angry with her that she beamed a bright smile back at him.

"What are you doing in the kitchen?" he asked.

"It's my punishment," Kate told him. "But I really don't mind working for Sister Sophia. I would rather bake than spin any old day!"

Peter nodded. "I am being punished, too, by having to do extra chores for the Brethren."

"Oh, Peter," Kate said, dismayed, "I am so sorry we got you into trouble."

The tall boy grinned ruefully. "It's not the first time my mischief-making cousin has gotten me into trouble. Anyway, I don't mind the work. One of my chores is to help Brother Joseph at the Community House. That's how I found out that Brother David is back."

"You mean David Zeisberger, the missionary?"

Peter nodded, and she caught the bright gleam of excitement in his eyes.

"Brother David is a very brave man, Kate. He traveled wilderness trails where no white man had ever gone before and lived in Indian villages. He was even adopted into the Onondaga tribe and given an Indian name." Peter's face beamed. "I'd like to be a missionary like him someday."

Kate shivered and exclaimed flatly, "Who would ever want to live in an Indian village and be adopted by an Indian tribe!"

The bright excitement left Peter's eyes, and the muscles around his mouth tightened. Without another word he gathered up his burlap sack and was on his way, leaving her standing there looking despairingly after him.

When she had hoped to make friends with Peter again, she had only angered him. But why couldn't he understand how she felt about Indians? How could the Moravians call redskins their brothers after what the Indians were doing to the settlers in the back country? With a sigh she wondered if she would ever understand Peter and if he would ever understand her. She gathered some sticks of wood and returned to the warm kitchen.

For the rest of the day she baked bread and helped Sister Sophia scrape and cut up vegetables for soup. As the day wore on, the gray stone walls of the Sisters' House seemed to close in on her, and the big stone house seemed more like a prison than ever. When Sister Sophia asked her to take some soup to Dr. Otto for his supper, she fairly flew to the wall peg for her cloak.

"You will find Brother Otto in the Apothecary," Sister Sophia said as she covered the small kettle of soup with a cloth. "Come back as soon as you can to help with the supper."

Kate took the kettle and hastened outside. The day was bright and sunny. Early November had come with its cold nights and frosty mornings. But the sun still had some warmth to it, and the afternoons were pleasant.

Kate walked down the lane to *Der Platz*, humming a Moravian hymn as she went. Listening to the Moravians singing all the time made her want to do the same thing, and she often caught herself humming one of their hymns.

The Apothecary was a small stone house on the square next to the Family House. Inside the shop Dr. John Matthew Otto was standing by a worktable, grinding dried herbs with a mortar and pestle.

Kate had never been inside an apothecary before. She stared for a long moment at the shelves laden with medicine bottles, beakers, brass scales, blood-letting knives, and pill rollers. Below the shelves were rows of drawers with the names of herbs and medicines printed on the outside of them. On another worktable were an assortment of surgical instruments, a basin, and a pitcher.

Dr. Otto looked up from his work and smiled when he saw the kettle of soup. He took it from Kate and set it on the hearthstone to keep warm. Reaching up, he brought down a tall glass jar from the shelf and took out several long strips of bark.

"Give this to Sister Sophia," he said. "She has always been partial to tea made from sassafras bark."

Kate took the bark. Its tangy fragrance reminded her of home and the sassafras tea Mama used to make for stomachaches. She thanked the doctor and left the shop.

As she was hurrying up the lane, a sudden gust of wind came up and she bent her head against it. Not looking where she was going, she did not see the passerby hurrying down the lane in the opposite direction. Not until she ran headlong into him and felt herself caught off balance by the impact, did she look up quickly.

A man dressed in a long black coat, Indian leggings, and shoepacs reached out to keep her from falling. "Whoa, there," he called out. When she was steady on her feet again, he said, "I don't believe that I have seen you here in Bethlehem before. My name is David Zeisberger."

Peter's hero!

"I—I didn't mean to bump into you," she stammered. "I guess I wasn't looking where I was going." Meekly she told him her name.

The missionary looked at her somewhat thoughtfully, then recalling her name, he said, "So you are the girl from Penn's Creek Settlement!" His tone softened and his smiling eyes turned sober. "Brother Joseph told me about your uncle bringing you here. While I was in the Wyoming Valley, I heard about that terrible raid."

Kate studied the man's craggy face, the large nose, and the wide upturned mouth that appeared to be smiling. But the deep wrinkles above his brows told her that he would understand her experience because he had seen hardship and suffering himself.

Her shyness melted away and she asked eagerly, "Were you at the Wyoming Valley when the Delawares and Shawnees brought in their captives?"

The missionary nodded, then listened intently while she described Benjamin.

"The Delawares and Shawnees keep their white captives well hidden in their villages," he told her. "They do not let us see them. But I will ask my Indian friends to be on the lookout for your brother."

At the missionary's words Kate felt a flicker of hope, the first hope she had since Benjamin was captured. "Oh, thank you, sir," she breathed. "That is good of you."

David Zeisberger was quiet for a moment, then his somber eyes brightened and he asked, "How do you like our town? It has a beautiful name, has it not?"

Without waiting for her answer, he pointed across the square to a log house perched on top of the hill above the springhouse. It had a long sloping roof and two doors which seemed to divide it into two parts, so that it had the appearance of two cabins stuck together.

"That was our first house," he told her. "It was in the smaller section of the house, the stable, that our town was officially named."

Kate looked surprised. "The town was named in a stable?"

David nodded. "Yes, it was, Kate." He paused, and his eyes took on a faraway look as he gazed over at the old house. "I was here at the time, a young man of twenty. I helped cut logs for that house. Come along. I'll show it to you and tell you the story of how Bethlehem got its name in a stable."

Forgetting that she should return to the kitchen as soon as she had finished her errand, Kate followed David Zeisberger across the square. She was eager to see the first house and to hear its story.

They stood for a moment looking at the old house, at its square-hewn logs that had weathered gray through the years. They peered through the windows, and David pointed out the living quarters and the stable. The old house looked as if it had not been lived in for a long time.

David Zeisberger said, "The story I'm going to tell you is our Christmas story, Kate. Every year it is told to the children. Come, let us sit here on the doorstep, and I'll tell it to you now."

They sat down on the flat stone that served as a doorstep, and David leaned back thoughtfully, cupping his hands around his bent knee. "It was fourteen years ago, in 1741, that this first house was built," he began. "In December of that year our leader and benefactor, Count Zinzendorf, whom we call Brother Ludwig, arrived in New York from Saxony to tour the Moravian and Indian settlements. He journeyed to Philadelphia, and from there he came north to our new settlement. He came on horseback, and with him and his party was his sixteen-year-old daughter, the beautiful Benigna. They stayed in the Community House, which was being built at that time."

David broke off for a moment, then went on with his story. "There were many workers here building the town. You might say the working group became the first citizens of Bethlehem. My father was a carpenter and my mother, Rosina, was here, too. Young as I was, and not skilled in any trade, I was a general helper wherever needed. We workers lived in this log house.

"The night before Christmas Count Zinzendorf and his daughter came to our house to help us celebrate the vigils of Christmas Eve. You see, we had no chapel then. But the women made the little house look festive. They decorated the room with pine and hemlock, as they did in the old country, and there was warm candlelight to lighten the happy faces.

"After a meal of venison and rabbit, Brother Ludwig stood up and began a hymn. More hymns followed. We were closing the service when the lowing of cattle could be heard from the adjoining stable. Brother Ludwig went into the stable, and we all followed. There among the animals he began to sing the old Epiphany hymn, 'Jesus, Call Thou Me.' We all joined in the singing. The words to that old hymn are:

> Not Jerusalem—lowly Bethlehem
> 'Twas that gave us Christ to save us;
> Not Jerusalem.
> Favored Bethlehem! honored is that name;
> Thence came Jesus to release us;
> Favored Bethlehem!

"After singing the hymn, Brother Ludwig turned to us and said, 'We shall call this place Bethlehem.'

"So here in a stable, like the one in Bethlehem of Judaea where the Christ child was born, our town got its name."

"Oh, 'tis a beautiful story," Kate exclaimed. "Now I know why Christmas means so very much to everyone living here."

"Especially to the children," David said, getting up from the stone and helping Kate to her feet. "That is why every Christmas we build the manger scene, or *Krippe,* as we call it, in a room in the Family House to remind the children of the night when the Christ child was born."

"The Christmas surprise," Kate murmured, remembering what Johanna had told her.

They walked back across the square together. David Zeisberger turned in at the Apothecary, and Kate hurried in the opposite direction, her long skirts billowing out around her as she ran. If Sister Magdalena saw me now, she'd have a fit, Kate thought, her heart knocking against her chest. She hoped Sister Sophia would not be too angry with her for being away so long.

When she arrived at the kitchen, the cook was busy preparing the supper. She glanced around and gave Kate a stern look.

"Can I naught trust you, my girl, to run a simple errand?"

"Oh, Sister Sophia, I'm sorry I am late," Kate said breathlessly, "but I met David Zeisberger, and he showed me the first house and told me the Christmas story."

"The Christmas story!" the cook exclaimed.

"Yes," Kate said, nodding vigorously, "about how Bethlehem got its name in a stable."

The stern look disappeared from Sister Sophia's round face. She had that same faraway look in her eyes as David Zeisberger had in his when he had gazed across the square at the first house.

"I, too, was here at the time," she murmured. "My young husband was alive and well then. He was helping to build the Community House. On Christmas Eve the Count, Brother Ludwig, and his beautiful young

81

daughter came to our first house to worship with us."

She gazed out the window in the direction of the old house, a little smile lifting the corners of her mouth. Forgotten now was the scolding she had intended for Kate. Her eyes were dreamy. Her voice was soft with remembering.

"Ah, yes, Kate, I was here, too."

9

Peter Turns
the Other Cheek

The bright fall days soon gave way to the solemn days of winter. The wild geese had flown south, and the gray skies were quiet once more. All the colored leaves had fallen, leaving the trees bare, gray skeletons. The November moon hung cold and aloof in the frosty sky.

Soon after the return of the two missionaries to Bethlehem, Brother Joseph sent the Indian scout, Brother Aaron, to the Wyoming Valley to find out what the Delawares and Shawnees were up to. The scout returned with news that Chief Teedyuscung's Delawares had swooped down on settlements along the Swatara and the Tulpehocken Creeks, west of Reading, killing thirteen settlers and destroying much property.

When Kate heard about the Swartara and Tulpehocken raids, it was like reliving the old horror. She
squeezed her eyes closed, but she could not shut from
her mind the six dark shapes slipping through the trees
of the clearing at Penn's Creek. She could not shut out
the quivering feathers in the scalp locks, the scarred
faces, and the yellow tongues of flames coming from
the cabin windows. That night in the garret dormitory
the nightmare returned, and she awoke screaming.
Johanna and the Sisters tried to comfort her.

News of other raids, burnings, and pillaging set off
panic among the settlers nearby, and the flight to
Bethlehem and its big stone buildings began. The
peaceful Moravian town soon became a crowded, noisy
town of old and new inhabitants.

Brother Timothy Horsfield, the justice of the peace,
posted guards at the three approaches of town, not in
fear of Indians, but in fear of the panic that might come
by the inrush of so many terror-stricken people seeking
refuge.

From the high windows of the Sisters' House Kate
and Johanna watched the groups of settlers shuffle
along the roads leading into town. They were weary
and travel worn, their clothes shabby and torn, the
children crying. Some had lost their shoes along the
way or had worn them bare on the rough trails and
hobbled down the lanes of town barefooted. The
refugees were lodged in the Brethren's House and at
the big gristmill. With so many extra mouths to feed,
the miller and his helpers worked long hours every day
to provide enough flour for bread.

During an evening *Singstunde* in the Chapel, the
Bishop told the Brethren and Sisters to sympathize

The congregation was solemn after Brother Joseph read the letter.

with the settlers who had come to Bethlehem for safety.

"We should appreciate the cause that scattered these poor souls and do whatever we can for them," Brother Joseph told the congregation. "Even though more come every day and it means a sacrifice to us all, Bethlehem will not turn a needy stranger away."

On November 20, Johanna wrote in her journal to her parents that a group of frightened settlers from Saucon Valley to the south had come around the mountain to Bethlehem. They had heard rumors of approaching Indians and had crowded into the Crown Inn across the river. Justice Horsfield exclaimed that he

scarcely knew how to provide for them all, but the next
Sunday, with a heavy rain beating against the chapel
windows, Brother Joseph preached the virtue of pa-
tience and the lesson of Job, who submitted to the test-
ing of the Lord. By rationing their food still further, the
Brethren were told to feed the hungry and to turn no
one away.

The same day that the Saucon Valley refugees came
to Bethlehem, an Indian runner brought Brother Joseph a letter from Martin Mack at Gnadenhuetten. The
Bishop read the letter to the congregation at the evening *Singstunde*. The missionary wrote that the entire
neighborhood was in a state of excitement because the
Delawares and Shawnees were trying to frighten the
Gnadenhuetten Indians into deserting the mission.
Many frightened Indians had already left Gnadenhuetten for the Wyoming Valley, the missionary wrote.
Only the sturdiest Christians remained, putting their
trust in the Savior. If worse came to worst, they would
cling together, and if must be, die together.

The congregation was solemn after Brother Joseph
read the letter. They were frightened at what the Delawares and Shawnees might do to Gnadenhuetten if all
the mission Indians did not desert. Kate was
frightened, too.

"But surely the Delawares and Shawnees will not attack a Moravian mission," Johanna tried to assure her
the next day, as the girls walked down to the mill on an
errand for Sister Sophia. "We Moravians have always
lived in peace with the Indians. They know we do not
believe in making war. Our muskets are used only for
hunting game."

Kate remembered the friendly missionaries at

Gnadenhuetten, who had given her and Uncle Josh food and shelter for the night. She thought about the youth, Joseph Sturgis, who had given her the moccasins. Oh, how she hoped Johanna was right!

The gristmill was a busy place these days. Not only were the miller and his helpers busy grinding grain to feed the refugees, but farmers in the valley who grew wheat, corn, and rye brought their grain to the mill to be ground into flour and cornmeal. That day several wagons from the Irish Settlement to the north of Bethlehem were drawn up in front of the mill. Peter and two other boys from the Brethren's House were helping the farmers unload sacks of grain from the wagons.

On the seat of one of the wagons sat a sulky youth, holding the reins. He was watching Peter drag the last sack of grain across the wagon bed. When the other boys and farmers disappeared into the mill with their loads, the boy on the wagon seat dropped the reins and jumped down from the wagon. He stepped in front of Peter as he was making his way toward the mill with his heavy sack.

"Injun lover!" the boy taunted.

Peter stopped and shifted the grain on his shoulder. He stared at the boy.

"My pa says a good Injun is a dead one. How come ye Moravians love 'em so much, or are ye on their side?"

Peter tried to sidestep the boy, but the taunting youth marched up to him and pushed the sack of grain off his shoulder. The bag burst and the grain spilled over the ground, making a yellow puddle in the middle of the mill yard.

Balling his fists, the Irish youth danced around

Peter, yelling, "Fight! Fight! Are ye Moravians too cowardly to fight?" He jabbed a fist into Peter's face and laughed, dancing around some more. "Fight, ye Injun lover. Fight!"

Peter's nose was bleeding, but he scarcely noticed it. His face was red and his gentle blue eyes now flashed with anger. Kate thought that now Peter would surely defend himself and fight back. But when the Irish boy made another jab at him with his fists, Peter only sidestepped, holding up his hands to ward off the blow.

"I will not fight you, so go away," Peter called out between clenched teeth.

"Injun lover! Coward!" the boy shouted.

Kate grasped Johanna's hand and squeezed it hard. "Why doesn't Peter defend himself?" she cried. "He's as big as that awful boy." Even though she was a girl, Kate felt like stepping up to the taunting boy herself and giving him a good punch in the nose. What was the matter with Peter?

Just then a group of ragged refugee children gathered around the two boys. "Fight! Fight!" they chanted, delighted at the excitement in front of the mill.

At the sound of the disturbance, Brother Joseph came out of the mill. A lanky farmer came hurrying after him. The two men separated the boys, and the Bishop handed Peter a large handkerchief for his nose.

"What is the meaning of this?" Brother Joseph asked sternly.

"My boy was only trying to defend himself," the farmer said.

"He was not!" Kate piped, her face flushed with anger. "He was the one who started the fight. Peter should have punched him right back."

Brother Joseph silenced her with a stern look. Then he turned to the Irish boy. "And why were you fighting with Peter?" he asked.

"I can answer that," the farmer spoke up again. "My son and all of us farmers from the Irish Settlement know how ye call Injuns yer brothers. We see yer Injun scouts going back and forth along the trail leading to the Wyoming Valley. And how can ye be so quiet and not afeared with all the Injun raids going on? I'll tell ye why. It's because ye are spies for the French and are in league with the French Injuns, that's why!"

Kate caught her breath and gaped at the farmer, then she glanced back at Brother Joseph.

The Bishop's level gaze met the farmer's. In a calm but firm voice he explained, "We are not spies for the French nor are we in league with the French Indians. Our scouts travel the trail to Wyoming to bring us news about the Delawares and Shawnees and to comfort our converted Indians who are being held there against their will. We are quiet because we believe in peace and set our hope in God, knowing no refuge under such circumstances but in him. And as God has counted all the hairs on our heads, not one of them shall be permitted to fall without his will."

The farmer grunted and led his son back to the wagon. Peter picked up the sack, scooping up as much grain into it as he could. He walked into the mill with Brother Joseph, and Kate noticed that the Bishop laid a comforting hand on the boy's shoulder.

The excitement over, the gathering of children wandered off. The girls got the sack of flour that Sister Sophia had sent them for and started up the hill, carrying the heavy sack between them.

They walked along in silence, but when they stopped halfway up the hill to rest, Kate shook her head and asked, "Why didn't Peter fight back? How could he just stand there when that farmer's son started the fight?"

Johanna drew in a long breath. "It was terribly hard for him not to fight back, Kate, but he didn't and I am proud of him. It showed courage not to fight back."

"Courage not to fight back!" Kate said with surprise. She would never understand these Moravians. She had always thought just the opposite, that it showed courage to fight back when someone picked on you.

She was about to open her mouth to say so when Johanna said, "I guess the Sermon on the Mount explains, better than I can, why Peter did not fight back. We have been taught those verses over and over again in school, so I know them by heart. One verse is: 'Ye have heard that it hath been said, An eye for an eye, and a tooth for a tooth: But I say unto you, That ye resist not evil: but whosoever shall smite thee on thy right cheek, turn to him the other also.' And in another verse Jesus tells us: 'Ye have heard that it hath been said, Thou shalt love thy neighbour, and hate thine enemy. But I say unto you, Love your enemies, bless them that curse you, do good to them that hate you, and pray for them which despitefully use you, and persecute you.'"

Johanna bent to grab her end of the sack. "So you see why Peter turned the other cheek and would not fight back? I'm proud of him for that, Kate. It takes real courage not to fight back when someone angers you."

Love your enemies . . . pray for them which despitefully use you, and persecute you. Did that mean Indians, too?

90

Kate frowned and reached for the other end of the sack. "Well, maybe the Sermon on the Mount can be meant for white folks," she conceded, "but the Bible doesn't say anything about loving Indians."

"The Bible says we must love our enemies, whoever they are," Johanna replied.

Kate looked grim and said slowly, "That's hard sometimes."

"Yes," Johanna agreed. "I know it is."

• • •

Three days later Johanna wrote in her journal: *Monday, November 24, 1755. Companies of militiamen marched through the town today. Peter learned at the Community House that the men were from New Jersey and were on their way to the Blue Mountain to scour the woods around Gnadenhuetten in search for hostile Indians. All day long the Jerseymen marched through Bethlehem from different parts of their colony. Some rode horses and others were on foot, with cockades bobbing jauntily on their hats and muskets leaning against their shoulders. With drums beating and fifes playing, they caused quite a sensation along our quiet lanes.*

Brother Joseph sent David Zeisberger to Gnadenhuetten to warn Martin Mack to keep our Moravian Indians in their houses so that they would not be mistaken for French Indians.

Like the men from the Irish Settlement, the Jerseymen looked askance at our peaceful people who went about their work as usual and refused to join them in the march. Only the refugees cheered them on, and many refugee men joined their ranks.

Kate told me that she felt like cheering the Jerseymen, too. She said at least they were doing something to try to stop the Indians from raiding more settlements. Sister Magdalena scolded her for running to the windows to watch the militiamen march by.

Work went on as usual even though drums beat and shots were fired into the air to demonstrate the intentions of the militiamen to fire upon any Indian they saw. Sister Magdalena said, "Thank goodness the Indians who are in town are shut up in the Indian House with the doors barred!" I quite agreed with her.

Finally, the last of the troops moved on through Bethlehem, and except for the excited refugees, peace and quiet settled once more over our town.

10

Gnadenhuetten

Kate was awakened early the next morning by the sound of horse's hoofs clattering up the lane. The rider seemed to be in a great hurry, she thought as she listened to the clip-clop of hoofbeats drum a staccato cadence on the stony road. Who could be riding into Bethlehem at this time of morning? It was dark outside with the stars still shining.

In the bed next to hers Johanna was sound asleep, but then Johanna could sleep through almost anything, Kate thought, smiling over at her friend. She propped herself up on her elbow and glanced around the quiet dormitory. All the other girls and Sisters appeared to be asleep, too. It seemed that she was the only one awakened by the horse and rider. She got out of bed and tiptoed quickly across the cold floorboards. From the dark recess of a dormer window, she gazed out at the starlit night.

Across the Bell House Square the dark silhouette of a man slipped wearily out of his saddle and made his way, as quickly as his stiff legs could take him, to the door of the Community House. Another shadow followed him, the shadow of a much larger man carrying a hooded lantern.

The rider hesitated at the door as the watchman held up his lantern. When he turned to talk to the watchman, his profile was visible against the lantern light. The craggy face and the large nose could belong to only one man—David Zeisberger. What is the missionary doing at the Community House at this hour? Kate wondered.

The door of the Community House opened and the missionary disappeared inside. The watchman continued on his way across the square. Moments later the bell in the Bell House tower rang the hour and Brother Matthias sang out:

> The clock is three! The blessed three do merit
> The best of praise from body, soul, and spirit.

Three o'clock in the morning! It was a strange time for Brother David to be returning from Gnadenhuetten. His message must be an urgent one to arouse the Bishop at this hour.

Just then one of the Sisters turned on her mattress and let out a long sigh. Kate waited for the woman to get settled, then, quiet as a mouse, she tiptoed back to her own bed.

Silence settled over the town once more, the only sound now being the rising wind that hummed around the corners of the dormer windows. Kate nestled down under her warm cover and was asleep almost at once. Two hours later she awoke as usual to the morning bell.

Instead of service in their own chapel that morning, the Deaconess announced that the Sisters would meet with the rest of the congregation in the big Chapel at the back of the Community House.

As the girls followed the others downstairs, Johanna told Kate, "When the Bishop and the Elders have the entire congregation meet in the Chapel this time of day, they usually have an important announcement to make."

Kate wondered if it could have anything to do with David Zeisberger's return to Bethlehem. But she didn't say anything to Johanna about what she had seen at three o'clock that morning. Soon enough they would find out.

The Sisters' House, the Bell House, the Chapel, and the Community House were all connected by long hallways and narrow doors so that the occupants could go from one building to the other without stepping outside. Now the procession of Sisters moved quickly through the dim halls of the Bell House to the Chapel door.

The Chapel was a long, plain room with windows set deep into its thick stone walls. There was no cross, no symbol to mark it as a Christian house of worship. There was no altar, only a communion table on a low platform in the middle of the west wall. Benches running north to south faced the platform where the Bishop stood. The men and boys entered from a door in the Community House and occupied the benches to the south. The women and girls entered through a door in the Bell House and occupied the benches to the north. The Elders and Deaconesses sat in the front rows.

When all were assembled, Brother Joseph opened the *Daily Text* and read to the congregation: " 'And Joseph saw his brethren, and he knew them, but made himself strange unto them, and spake roughly unto them. . . .' "

The Bishop looked up at the anxious faces before him and said, "Thus, my Brethren and Sisters, our Lord sometimes deals roughly with us and makes himself strange, but we know his heart."

There was a stir in the congregation. Everyone sensed that something was disturbing their Bishop. They waited for his next words.

In a solemn voice Brother Joseph said, "Yesterday I sent Brother David Zeisberger to Gnadenhuetten. His mission was to warn Brother Martin Mack to keep our Moravian Indians in their houses because the militiamen were seeking out French Indians in the vicinity and might mistake our converted Brethren for hostile Indians. On the way Brother David was detained by a company of Jerseymen who accused him of going to Gnadenhuetten to alarm the French sympathizers about their coming. It took Brother David a long time to reason with the militiamen that there were no French sympathizers at Gnadenhuetten.

"At last they permitted him to ride on, but he did not reach the mission until evening came on. He delivered my message to Martin Mack and was on his way across the river to spend the night at the mission farm when he heard gunshots, but thought nothing of it because of the militiamen in the forest.

"However, he soon found out that it was not the Jerseymen doing the shooting. Two missionaries from the mission farm, Joachim Sensemann and George Partsch, met him on the east bank of the river and told him that the French Indians were burning the mission farm and massacring the people there. The two men were on their way to the mission house to alert Martin Mack. They told Brother David to turn back and take the dreadful news to Bethlehem."

At the Bishop's words, the congregation sucked in their breath in audible shock. A low moan of despair rippled through the Chapel. Every back stiffened visibly as Brother Joseph continued.

"There was nothing for Brother David to do but to set out in the darkness on his weary horse and return to Bethlehem. On the way he met the Jerseymen again at their camp in the mountain pass. When they heard the news of the Indian raid at Gnadenhuetten, they told Brother David that now they know we Moravians are not spies nor in league with the French Indians. That much good came out of it."

Brother Joseph paused. His voice trembled when he next spoke. "Oh, my Brethren, 'tis bitter news I bring you. We must pray for the souls of those who lost their lives and for those of our people who have witnessed this terrible thing."

Kate felt a knot of fear grow tight in her stomach. She clutched the bench beneath her until her hands ached. She thought about the flaxen-haired youth, Joseph Sturgis, who had given her the moccasins. Had he been massacred with the others at the mission farm?

The day was one of mourning. The people of Bethlehem put aside their daily tasks and gathered at *Der Platz* to await the refugees from Gnadenhuetten.

Late in the morning the first refugee, Peter Worbas, arrived. His eyes stark, his face ashen, he slid off his horse in front of the Apothecary and literally fell into Dr. Otto's arms. While the doctor administered to him, Peter Worbas told what he had seen, the words tumbling from his lips in short, painful gasps.

He had been ill with a fever and had not joined the others for supper last evening but had witnessed the terrible scene from the window of his sickroom. Before the Indians burned the building he was in, he leaped out the window and fled into the woods by the creek. There he had found a stray horse and had ridden all night to reach Bethlehem.

In the afternoon Joachim Sensemann walked wearily into Bethlehem with about thirty Gnadenhuetten Indians who had escaped because they were at the new mission on the east side of the river. Later in the day Martin Mack and his wife arrived with forty more Indians. The seventy Indians were sheltered in the Indian House across the creek.

Kate stood in the square with the others, watching anxiously as the survivors straggled into Bethlehem. She kept looking for a stocky youth with flaxen hair. She asked about Joseph, but no one seemed to know what had happened to him. Her hands felt icy as she clutched them together and wondered if Joseph had survived the massacre.

She had almost given up hope for him when the next day the last three survivors—a young man and woman and a grown boy—were seen approaching the town. Everyone met in the square again to greet the weary travelers. They looked to be half alive, dragging one foot after the other. The youth was walking with a limp. His clothes were torn and dusty, and there was a bloodstained cloth wrapped around his head and down across his cheeks. Beneath the cloth showed long wisps of yellow hair.

Joseph Sturgis! She was sure it was Joseph. And he was alive!

She gave a cry of relief when she saw him. "Joseph! Joseph Sturgis!"

The youth looked up at the sound of his name. With dazed eyes, he stared at her as if she were a stranger. Then remembering the girl he had given the moccasins to, his thin lips lifted into a bleak wisp of a smile.

Dr. Otto, who had been administering to the other refugees, hurried out of the Apothecary and led the wounded boy inside. That night Joseph, his face freshly bandaged where a bullet had grazed his cheek, was housed in the Brethren's House, where he shared a bed with Peter.

The next day when Peter filled their woodbox, he told the girls that Joseph was still asleep. "He's so exhausted that he'll probably sleep all day," Peter said.

Before he left, he told them the latest news from the Community House. "I heard Brother Joseph say that because of the massacre at Gnadenhuetten, the children from the school and nursery at Nazareth will be moved to Bethlehem."

Johanna looked around anxiously. "Our town is so crowded now with refugees, where will Brother Joseph put them all?"

"The children from Nazareth will be housed with our children in the Family House," Peter replied. "Brother Joseph will not turn anyone away, especially little children."

The governor sent rangers to build a stockade.

The days that followed the raid at Gnadenhuetten were anxious ones. After hearing about the massacre at the mission farm, the leaders at the Irish Settlement, like the Jerseymen, knew that the Brethren were not spies nor allied in any way with the French and Indians. They asked Brother Joseph if their women and children could come to Bethlehem should their settlement be attacked. Again Brother Joseph offered sanctuary.

Rations were again cut in preparation for the children's coming. Now at every meal, as Kate glanced down at the small portion of food on her plate, she wondered if she would ever feel full again. It was not an unusual occurrence to go to bed every night with a hollow feeling in her stomach.

Hearing of the massacre at Gnadenhuetten and fearing that Bethlehem might be in danger, Governor Morris of Pennsylvania sent a troop of rangers to put up defenses. A stockade, with watchtowers at the corners, was to be built along the north and west sides of the central buildings, and all the windows of the lower floors of the buildings were to be boarded. Justice Horsfield agreed with the governor that the best defense would be to keep proper watches day and night, so a regular system of watchmen was established.

"You should feel safe now with all the defenses going up," Peter told the girls as they strolled around town to watch the rangers start work on the stockade. He stepped beside Kate and looked down at her with eyes full of tenderness and concern, as if for the first time he really understood and cared about how frightened she was.

Kate's throat felt tight with affection and gratitude. She longed to put her hand in his, to let him know how much she appreciated his concern, but here in Bethlehem it would not be the proper thing to do. They should not even be walking together along the same path. Like a proper Moravian girl, but with an inward sigh, she looked down demurely, letting her lashes veil the gratefulness that shone in her eyes.

Peter's confidence in Bethlehem's security was short-lived, however. That same evening at the *Singstunde* Augustus, one of the Indians quartered at the Indian House, burst into the Chapel and interrupted the service. He reported that in the soft owl light strange Indians were seen skulking in the woods in back of the house. Augustus was fairly shaking when he told of the threats that had been made by one of the prowlers who had ventured within earshot of the Indian House.

Brother Joseph immediately brought the service to a close. The night watch was doubled and posted at the five corners of the town. It was agreed that if one of the men on watch saw strange Indians approach the town, he should discharge his musket as a signal. The other watchmen would do the same to warn the Indians that the town was well guarded. By doing so, the Brethren hoped to discourage any mischief the prowling Indians had planned and to avoid possible bloodshed.

In the Sisters' House that night the warden locked the door with a large iron key. She looked into the leather fire buckets hanging on their pegs in the entrance hall to see that they were filled, then chose two Sisters for the night watch.

Kate was getting ready for bed when she heard the shot ring out. It was followed by several other shots. She stiffened and felt a quick, hot throb of fear. She flew to the windows with the Sisters and girls to peer out into the night. The bell rang a general alarm. From the Brethren's House ran a group of men assigned to remain awake for such an emergency. They lined up in front of the Bell House Square to protect the Community House and the Sisters' House. Kate wondered how they were going to do this with no muskets in their hands.

After several long agonizing minutes, Brother Matthias came to the door of the Sisters' House and talked with the Sisters on watch. It was a relief to learn that one of the nervous watchmen had accidentally discharged his rifle. But an uneasy night followed, and nearly all the men in Bethlehem remained up and watchful.

The Sisters and girls returned to their beds, but Kate could not sleep. The quiet darkness of the dormitory seemed to close in and smother her. Panic swept over her, and she felt like screaming with all the breath she had. Uncle Josh and Brother Joseph and Peter had been wrong. And Johanna had been wrong, too, thinking that the Delawares and Shawnees would not attack the peaceful Moravians. Bethlehem was no safer now than Penn's Creek or Gnadenhuetten or any other settlement raided by the Indians.

That night she dreamed again of scarred, painted faces, of flames licking up the sides of the cabin, of the suffocating darkness of the root cellar.

11

Wagonloads of Children

On the first day of December the children from Nazareth arrived. They came in five canvas-covered wagons drawn by oxen. The wagons were escorted by a small band of Moravian Indians, led by the scar-faced scout, Brother Aaron.

Inhabitants of Bethlehem and refugees alike stopped their work to peer curiously out of doorways and second-story windows at the small ox-drawn wagons.

Kate and the girls were gathering the last of the herbs in the garden behind the Brethren's House. They paused in their gathering to listen to the drivers call for the oxen to halt. Mingled with the cries of the drivers came the sound of children's voices singing. In the distance the thin, high voices sounded like little bells tinkling on the frosty air.

The girls hurried to the front of the Brethren's House

just in time to see the last wagon in line draw to a stop in front of the Family House. Eagerly small faces peered out through the canvas at the buildings around them.

"The children were told they are on holiday and have come to Bethlehem to spend the Christmas season here," Anna Catherine explained. "That's why they are so happy."

"And Sister Magdalena said they must never, never be told about the danger," Regina added soberly. "I hope they don't wonder about the muskets the watchmen are carrying or the boarded windows in the Family House."

Johanna shook her head. "They probably think the men who are carrying muskets are going hunting for game, and they won't think it strange that the first-floor windows in the Family House are boarded. That is where the Christmas surprise is going to be."

Johanna paused, then chattered on with a reminiscent sparkle in her eyes. "Remember, as small girls, how mysterious and wonderful it all was? The door was locked and the blinds were closed in the room where the Christmas surprise was being made. But from windows on the second floor we could see the men dragging in evergreen boughs from the woods and the Sisters carrying mysterious boxes and baskets of all sizes and shapes into the Family House. That is what's in these children's minds now; I'm sure of it."

Kate frowned, hardly daring to ask, "With the Indian danger and everybody busy with the refugees, will there still be time for the Christmas surprise this year?"

Anna Catherine was startled by Kate's question. "Of

course there will be! Sister Esther said that this year, more than ever, the children must have their Christmas surprise."

Kate looked back at the wagons where the children were still singing and laughing, and her own face relaxed into a smile. She was glad that they would be having their Christmas surprise this year, and she was relieved that the children did not wonder about the watchmen with muskets or the barricaded houses. As Sister Magdalena had said, they must not know about the danger.

Brother Aaron was helping the children off the wagons. Kate was surprised at how gentle he was with them. Even the smallest children threw their arms around him and squealed with delight as he lifted them down. His ugly, scarred face did not seem to bother them at all.

"Look, there's Brother Joseph coming out of the Family House," Regina said, pointing.

The girls watched the portly man, dressed as always in his plain brown suit, walking up the wagons to greet the children. They stopped singing and cried out with joy, "Brother Joseph! Brother Joseph!"

"They remember him because of the love feasts they have when he comes to Nazareth to visit their school," Johanna told Kate.

"Welcome to Bethlehem, my children," Brother Joseph called out. His ruddy face shone with happiness that all the the wagons with the children had arrived safely. Gathering the smaller children around him, he led them into the Family House where they would occupy the nursery.

The older children did not follow as quietly. Now that

they had arrived at the Christmas town, they were more excited than ever. The girls giggled as they watched the Sisters trying to organize the flight from the wagons and to still the shrill voices.

From behind windows and open doorways, strained faces relaxed and smiles crept on lips that had been saddened these long trying days. The arrival of the children from Nazareth and their happy voices had brought a note of cheer to the anxious town.

The children took innocent delight at the fuss being made over them. They were looking forward to the hot meal that was promised at their arrival and to the other treats in store for them here in Bethlehem.

One special treat came the very next day when they were taken across *Der Platz* to see the first house. The older girls helped the Sisters march the children across the square, where David Zeisberger met them. Brother David explained about the first house, then told them the story of the first Christmas in Bethlehem, just as he had told it to Kate.

For a few moments, as Kate listened to the story again, the ragged refugees, the watchmen with muskets, and the ugly raw logs of the stockade were forgotten and Bethlehem was the quiet, peaceful settlement that it had once been.

Snowflakes began to drift down on the old house as Brother David finished his story, just as they had that first Christmas Eve. Cheeks reddened with the cold, the children fled across the square to the warmth of the Family House, where they had been promised a love feast.

A short while later, the girls were helping to load trays with freshly baked buns, still warm from the oven. Always hungry now, Kate could hardly wait to bite into her bun. But the children and Sisters had to be served first.

As the girls moved among the children with their trays, Anna Catherine explained to Kate, "We always have love feasts to welcome our people to Bethlehem, and this one is to welcome the children of Nazareth."

And how they loved it! While the girls passed the buns, the Sisters helped the younger ones with mugs of weak, sugared tea. When every last crumb had been eaten and every last drop of tea drunk, one of the Sisters walked over to the spinet and led them in singing the old hymn which inspired Count Zinzendorf to name the little settlement Bethlehem.

Not Jerusalem—lowly Bethlehem
'Twas that gave us Christ to save us. . . .

When the children finished singing the hymn, the Sister asked, "Now how would you like to sing your favorite hymn, 'Morning Star'?"

The children danced up and down and clapped their hands. The Sister struck the chord and they came to attention. Little boys in homespun jackets and knee breeches and the girls, dressed like miniature Sisters in long dresses and little white caps, started to sing the hymn that they all knew and loved so well.

Morning Star, O cheering sight!
Ere thou cam'st how dark earth's night.
Jesus mine, in me shine;
Fill my heart with light divine.

As Kate looked around the gathering of singing children, she noticed the round, dusky face of an Indian boy. His large, black eyes were solemn as he watched the other children, who were bubbling over with happy enthusiasm. He reminded Kate of a startled young deer she had once come upon suddenly in the pines by their clearing.

She judged the Indian boy to be about the same age as Benjamin. And her heart filled with sadness as she thought about the happy little boy that October day on their way to the walnut grove. He, too, had reminded her of a yearling deer as he capered about through the trees, stopping to examine an interesting stone or a piece of wood.

Kate bit her lip and turned away from the Indian child. But as she turned and walked to the window, she could feel his dark, solemn eyes follow her.

Outside the snow was falling steadily. Already it had covered the lane and had laid a white mantle on the shingled roof of the first house. Between snowy banks the creek had the sullen look of tarnished pewter. Dusk deepened between the trees. Darkness would come early today.

She shivered and turned back to the warm candlelight and the happy voices.

12

The Danger

The carding room in the Sisters' House was a busy place in the days that followed. The girls helped Sister Esther card more wool, then twist it into fluffy balls of woolly sheep.

"With the children from Nazareth here, we have to make many more sheep if each child is to get one on Christmas day," Sister Esther reminded the girls. "And not only do we have to make them for our own children but for the refugee children as well. Poor *Kinder*, it may be the only Christmas gift they get."

While Sister Esther and the girls worked on their woolly sheep, the men found time to carve more wooden shepherds for the Christmas crib. Peter, Joseph Sturgis, and the older boys ventured into the woods across the creek for rocks and moss and evergreen boughs. Several scouts from the Indian House went with them to make sure there were no French Indians lurking about.

All this preparation made much activity in the first-floor room of the Family House as the crib began to take shape. It was difficult for the curious children not to peek. One day two boys were caught at the keyhole and were sent scooting up the stairs to the nursery by one of the Sisters.

Meanwhile, more refugees came to Bethlehem from raids at nearby settlements. On December 10 three wagons from the mill left Bethlehem and were on their way to the Brodhead Settlement to get much needed grain when they met a company of half-dressed women and children on the road. The wagons brought the pitiable refugees to Bethlehem, where they were given warm clothing and food.

Every day now the Indians from the Indian House went hunting. They had to venture deep into the forest to get meat for the hungry town. Usually they returned with squirrels, rabbits, and other small game. Sometimes they came back with deer, and one day an Indian shot a bear. It was good to eat fresh meat again, even if everyone's portion was small.

Each day Kate and Johanna would look for Peter as he made his rounds to fill the woodboxes. Sometimes, when the weather was good, they would slip out of the Sisters' House and wait for him in the shelter of one of the big stone buttresses. They were eager for the scraps of news he brought them from the Community House.

One day Peter had exciting news. "Benjamin Franklin has just arrived in Bethlehem from Philadelphia," he told the girls. "He has been commissioned by

Governor Morris to build defenses in the back country. He and two other commissioners, with a guard of fifty men, are to spend the night at the Crown Inn across the river."

That same night Brother Joseph called the Bethlehem congregation together and told them that the commissioners were to supervise the building of a chain of forts along the passes in the Blue Mountain between the Delaware and the Susquehanna rivers. The forts were to be built so that the settlers could gather in them for protection during Indian raids. The work was to begin that winter.

When several Brethren in the congregation suggested that the Bishop ask Mr. Franklin for guns and men to protect Bethlehem. Brother Joseph replied, "We have our own watchmen to protect us. We do not trust in weapons nor in soldiers, for we know for certain that if the Lord will have us suffer, no weapons will keep us free. If he will have us safe, nothing will be able to hurt us in the least."

The next day, after Mr. Franklin and the commissioners left Bethlehem, it began to snow again. All day a white curtain of whirling flakes hid the river from view and blurred the big stone buildings.

"We have to watch carefully for Peter," Johanna said, looking out the window by the door. "It is too cold to stand by the buttress to wait for him."

"Look, here he comes now!" Kate said, pointing to a gray form trudging through the drifts. They snatched up their cloaks and made their way out of the Sisters' House to meet him.

One look at Peter's cold, pinched face told them that he had something on his mind. But it was not until he had filled the woodbox that he told them what it was.

"Soon after the commissioners left," he said, "an Indian runner came to the Community House with news that the Delawares and Shawnees are planning to attack Bethlehem."

The girls stared at the boy with wide, frightened eyes.

Peter added hastily, "But Brother David thinks it may be just a threat to frighten our Indians into leaving Bethlehem and joining the French at Wyoming."

"Our faithful Indians will never leave Bethlehem," Johanna said, brushing the snowflakes from her cloak with a mittened hand. "Oh, I do hope that it keeps snowing and snowing and snowing so that the drifts pile high and the French Indians can't attack."

With this disturbing news, the workmen hurriedly finished the stockade with its watchtowers at the corners. More windows in the houses were boarded, even those in the upper stories.

One afternoon while the girls were having vesper hour, a carpenter arrived at their room to board their second-story window. The four girls were sitting at the table, enjoying cups of weak tea, when he arrived. As they watched him work, Anna Catherine asked curiously, "Why are you boarding only the bottom half of the window, Brother Huber?"

The carpenter took a nail from between his lips, and as he pounded it into the board and window frame, he replied, "You don't need the entire window boarded up. From the ground below the range of bullets fired up at the top of the window would be well above the heads of all who are in the room. Yet enough light can enter above the sash so that you can see. And if you are careful, you can look out the top half."

"That's a clever idea, Brother Huber!" exclaimed Johanna.

Clever or not, Kate did not like the idea of having even the bottom half of their window boarded. It made the danger seem that much closer. She wished that Brother Joseph had listened to the Brethren who had wanted to ask Mr. Franklin for men and weapons to defend the town.

Great care was taken to prevent panic among the refugees and to keep the news of a possible Indian attack from the children. The Brothers and Sisters went about their chores as usual in calm and peace, singing their familiar hymns as they worked. They never discussed the danger. Not even among themselves.

With Christmas so near, Sister Esther and the girls hurriedly finished the last of the woolly sheep. At school in the Bell House the girls were now busy printing verses that would be hung on the greens for Christmas day.

Kate had mastered the art of penmanship, and now her quill pen performed the ornamental lettering without spattering gobs of ink all over her paper. In fact, she was grateful to be hard at work printing the little verses for the children because it took her mind off the danger.

Every afternoon at vesper hour the girls stood on tiptoes to look through the upper half of their boarded window. The lamb weather vane on top of the Bell House roof now pointed steadily north and had icicles hanging from its sides. Even though there had been no more snow, the world was white and bleak, with bitter winds that swayed the tallest trees mournfully to and fro. The lanes in town were deserted. All who did not have to be out in the cold stayed inside by their fireplaces and tile stoves.

With concern on her usually cheerful face, Johanna said, "I still keep praying for a big blizzard that will last all winter long."

"I keep praying for one, too," replied Regina.

Each day the sky was gray and threatening, and it looked as if the girls' prayers would be answered. But there was no more heavy snow, and Peter informed them that the roads and trails leading into town were open.

Two days before Christmas Sister Esther delivered the woolly sheep to the Family House. When she returned from her errand, she told the girls that the Christmas crib was at last completed. Her eyes lit up when she described it. "With all our woolly sheep and the new shepherds the Brethren have made, it will be the largest *Krippe* and the best Christmas surprise ever!"

The next morning the girls could hardly wait to tell Peter what Sister Esther had said about the crib. When they saw him plodding up the lane with his heavy sack, they ran to meet him.

"Peter!" Kate called. "Sister Esther said the Christmas surprise is completed."

"And she said it is the largest and the best *Krippe* ever!" Johanna added.

Peter twisted the sack of wood off his back and muttered, "I hope the children will be able to see it." He sucked in his breath quickly as if he regretted the words that had slipped between his lips.

Johanna gave her cousin a puzzled look. "What do

you mean, Peter. Of course the children will see it on Christmas morning."

Peter avoided their inquiring eyes and absent-mindedly started to take sticks of wood out of his sack. What is the matter with him today, Kate wondered as she watched him pile the wood in the middle of the snowy path instead of in the woodbox.

Johanna stamped her cold feet on the frozen snow. "What did you *mean* by saying that, Peter?" she asked again.

Peter still did not answer. He put the last pieces of wood down on the path and was about to flee with his sack when Kate reached out and grabbed the sleeve of his coat. "Tell us, Peter," she pleaded.

The boy turned slowly. He looked down at his snowy boots as if he were studying them intently. Finally he said, "Oh—all right—I'll tell you. It's just that I didn't want to frighten you with the news. But I suppose you'll hear about it anyway."

Lowering his sack to the ground, he spoke almost in a whisper. "Brother Aaron has been to the Wyoming Valley. He just returned to warn us that what the Indian runner had told us was true. A band of Delawares and Shawnees are planning a raid on Bethlehem. Brother Aaron learned that they plan to attack on Christmas Eve."

Johanna's mouth flew open in startled protest. "But that's tonight!"

"I know," Peter said, swallowing hard. "But that's what Brother Aaron said. The Indians plan to attack on the eve of what they call the white man's 'Great Day'—Christmas." He raised his arms and let them flop against his heavy coat. There was nothing he could do or say to make them feel any better.

As if in a trance, Kate reached for the wood, but Peter took the sticks from her and put them in the box by the door. Before he left, he straightened his shoulders and told them, "Don't worry. The Brethren will be keeping watch tonight—and I'll be with them."

He sounded very grown-up as he spoke those last words. Slinging the sack over his shoulder, he was off in long strides down the frozen path.

Kate wanted to hurry after him, to grasp his hand, and to tell him to be careful. But instead, she found herself following Johanna into the Sisters' House.

Leaning against the stone wall of the entrance hall, Johanna took a deep, quivering breath. "Oh, Kate, I wish that we hadn't forced Peter to tell us, then we wouldn't know and be so frightened."

But Kate shook her head. " 'Tis better to know and not to be taken by surprise, Johanna. Maybe that's why Peter gave in so easily and did tell us."

A creak on the stairs made both girls whirl around. Sister Magdalena, dressed in her heavy cloak, was descending the long stairway. Her face seemed paler and sterner than usual as she looked down at the two girls.

"The Sister who is in charge of the nursery has come down with the ague," she said in crisp tones. "The Deaconess is sending me to the Family House to take her place."

Before she left, Sister Magdalena gave each girl a warning look. "I hope you are not planning to go outside in this cold weather. There is so much chills and fever about. Promise you will stay inside today unless you are sent on an errand."

Kate knew that it was not just the cold weather and the chills and fever that Sister Magdalena was warning them about. She nodded and quickly lowered her eyes so that the Sister could not see the fear in them.

Johanna ran to open the door. "We promise," she called out as Sister Magdalena stepped over the threshold and started down the path to the lane.

The long day stretched out before them. Even though it was the day before Christmas and everyone should be happy, a grim expectation hung over the town. The danger that everyone had coped with so calmly now seemed suddenly very real and almost too much to bear.

The Sisters went quietly about their work, forgetting to sing at their chores. The tutoress in the schoolroom did not seem to notice when the girls made mistakes in their ciphering. Even Johanna's cheerful face was sullen most of the day.

Kate longed to be alone. At Penn's Creek when something was troubling her, she would go for a walk in the woods where she could be by herself to think things out. But here in Bethlehem the Sisters and girls worked together, ate together, and even relaxed together. Except to run an errand, it was frowned upon to go off on one's own.

As the day wore on, Kate grew desperate. During vesper hour she did not return to the room with the other girls but slipped off by herself down the dim hallway of the Bell House.

Something drew her to the Chapel door. It stood open invitingly and she paused a moment to peer inside. She was relieved that the Chapel was empty and sank down on a bench in the back.

The big room that was so plain before was now transformed for Christmas. Hemlock garlands, interwoven with glossy leaves of laurel, were hung around the sides of the room along with wreathes of pine. The artist, Valentine Haidt, who had a studio in Justice Horsfield's house, had painted the nativity scene which hung on the wall above the communion table. The Deaconess had told them that it was Brother Valentine's Christmas gift to the town he loved.

How different Christmas in Bethlehem was from the simple celebration at Penn's Creek! Kate thought about the little clearing now deserted, its charred ruins covered with snow. She thought about the two recent graves in the little grove of hemlocks, their mounds also snow-covered. She thought about Benjamin, who would be spending his Christmas in some Indian village far away.

A flame of anger flashed through her cold body. It was all the Indians' fault! She hated them for what they did to her parents, to her brother, to the missionaries at Gnadenhuetten, and for what they threatened to do this Christmas Eve to Bethlehem.

She buried her face in her hands. For several long minutes she sat there, trembling with the thought of it. She did not see the door at the far end of the room opening nor the dark figure, like a moving shadow, making its way across the Chapel.

Not until a hand reached out to touch her bent shoulder did she look up. She gave a start at the face bending over her.

13

Christmas Eve

"**B**rother Joseph!" she gasped, surprised that she had not heard the Bishop come across the Chapel. But like so many big men, he walked with a soft tread. She blinked troubled eyes at him, fearful of what he would say at finding her here alone.

But Brother Joseph did not scold, even though his face was grim. He simply asked, "You are frightened, my child? Is that why you have come to the Chapel alone?"

Kate nodded, then lowered her eyes. She wished the shaking inside her would stop.

The Bishop sat down beside her, and the bench gave a sharp groan under his weight. The row of buttons that fastened together his plain brown coat strained as he leaned over.

"We must put our trust in the Lord," he said calmly. "Remember this, my child, 'Except the Lord keep the city, the watchman waketh but in vain.'"

Was Brother Joseph thinking of Bethlehem on this Christmas Eve when he quoted that passage from the Scriptures? Kate wondered. When the Bishop next spoke, she was surprised at how confident he sounded.

"Tomorrow, to usher in the dawn, the trombone choir will play three Christmas chorales from the roof of the Brethren's House. Afterward, we can all rejoice, and the children can have their Christmas surprise."

Tomorrow ... the trombone choir will play three Christmas chorales .... Oh, if it could be so and everyone in Bethlehem would hear the trombones and the children would have their Christmas surprise! But a second later her hopes fell. How could it be, with the Indians attacking tonight?

Brother Joseph helped her up from the bench and walked with her back through the Bell House. They walked in silence, their footsteps making soft echoes in the hollow hallway. When they reached the Sisters' House, Brother Joseph said, "I am going to ask the Deaconess to send you to the Family House." He paused, and the creases in his cheeks deepened into smile lines. "The children will be excited, thinking about their Christmas surprise tomorrow. Sister Magdalena will have her hands full and may need a young girl's help to settle them."

Kate knew that Sister Magdalena was capable of settling anyone, even an unruly child, and the Bishop knew it too. He also knew that there was nothing like the exuberant joy of little children on Christmas Eve to cheer one up. Kate cast a grateful glance at the big man walking by her side. Now she knew what Sister Sophia meant when she said that Brother Joseph was everyone's brother.

While the Bishop went to talk to the Deaconess, Kate hurried to the girls' room, where she found Johanna sitting in her chair reading her Bible. Kate picked up her own leather-bound Bible. It was her only possession from home, and she did not wish to leave it behind. Besides, it would be a great comfort to have her mother's Bible close to her through the long night.

While she waited for the Deaconess' permission to leave, Kate sat with Johanna and told her about meeting Brother Joseph in the Chapel. "Oh, Johanna, it will be fun being with the children, but I wish we could go together."

At that moment the Deaconess arrived to see Kate off. As Kate got up to leave, Johanna leaped up from her chair. Quickly she tied her cap strings and jerked her apron around to straighten it. As she did so, she blurted out, "I'd like to go with Kate to help with the children!"

At such an outburst the Deaconess pulled down the corners of her mouth in disapproval, but seeing the earnest twinkle in the girl's eyes, her own face brightened and she nodded her approval. Johanna, with her fun-loving ways, might be the best girl of all to be with the children during this night of danger.

In parting she told the girls, "You must go about your tasks as usual and must keep even a hint of the danger from the children. Now Godspeed until morning."

The girls bundled their Bibles under their woolen cloaks and made their way down the hill to the square.

The only people they saw on this cold afternoon were a little knot of refugees with blankets over their heads and shoulders, talking in muffled tones to one of the watchmen.

The girls hurried past the Apothecary to the stone house next door. A young Sister, not much older than they, answered the door of the Family House and guided them to the nursery, where Sister Magdalena was seated at the spinet. The children were gathered around her, practicing the Christmas carols that they were to sing at the children's love feast the next day. Sister Magdalena was surprised to see the girls but was pleased to have extra help and set them busy at once teaching the younger children the words of the carols they were singing.

> Morning Star, O cheering sight!
> Ere thou cam'st how dark the night. . . .

Kate wondered if the morning star would be a cheering sight over Bethlehem the next morning, or would it be shining down on a burning town. She caught her lip between her teeth to keep from trembling. She must not let the children sense her fear. In as steady a voice as she could manage, she led them in singing the beloved carol.

When they had finished practicing the carols, Sister Magdalena arose from the spinet and walked over to a shadowy corner of the room. When she rejoined the group of children, she was leading the Indian boy by the hand. She led the child over to where the two girls were standing.

"This is Nathan," she told them, looking steadily at Kate as she spoke. "The Delaware Indian village that was his home was raided and burned by English soldiers, and both his parents were killed. But Nathan miraculously escaped and was found by one of our missionaries who brought him to the children's school in Nazareth. He is not used to being around so many white children and is homesick for his home and his parents. Perhaps you can give him a little extra attention."

Kate stared down at the boy, who looked back at her with those same dark sober eyes. Sister Magdalena wanted her to care for an Indian child!

She turned away, her throat tight. Let Johanna take charge of Nathan. Johanna wouldn't mind caring for an Indian boy. Kate quickly turned her attention to the other children, who were pelting the Sisters with questions.

"Why do we have to wait 'til tommorrow to see the Christmas surprise?"

"Why can't we see it tonight?"

"When will tomorrow be?"

Sister Magdalena clapped her hands for silence. "You may see the Christmas surprise as soon as breakfast is over tomorrow."

A groan went around the circle of children. A boy sitting on the spinet bench jumped up and grumbled, "Aw, we *would* have to wait until after breakfast tomorrow!" Seeing Sister Magdalena's disapproving frown, he quickly changed the subject and in the next breath shouted, "Let's have a game of hide-and-seek. I'll be 'it' first."

Forgetting about the Christmas surprise for the moment, the other children ran to find hiding places in the dark corners of the room. Johanna led the Indian boy into the game by hiding him behind her and making motions that he should be quiet. The spinet bench was base, and with shrieks and wild scrambling the children rushed to it so that they would not be caught.

Sister Magdalena did not seem to notice the noise and confusion. Calmly, as if she were in her own quiet room in the Sisters' House, she opened her sewing bag and took out a bit of embroidery to work on. Surprisingly, she did not scold nor try to quiet the children. Could she be wanting them to have one last good time while they can? Kate wondered.

At last supper hour came, and afterwards the children were told that they must get ready for bed. Tomorrow would be a big day for them. The older children groaned in protest, but the Sisters hustled them up the narrow stairs to the dormitory on the top floor.

Kate and Johanna helped get the younger children into their linen nightshirts. There was quite a rustling around on the beds until Sister Magdalena warned, "If you do not go to sleep at once, you may not hear the morning bell and you may be late for the Christmas surprise." Not one of them wanted that to happen, so they finally settled down and closed their eyes.

After all the children were settled, the girls got ready for bed themselves. Johanna blew out their candle and curled up with a sleepy sigh in her feather tick. Kate snuggled under her covers and looked out one of the little dark windows. A bright star blinked in the Christmas sky. At the opposite end of the room, where Sister Magdalena kept watch, blinked the linseed oil lamp that would burn through the night. Its light threw thin shadows over the sleeping children.

Outside the bell rang the hour, and Brother Matthias sang out:

Past eight o'clock! O Bethlehem, do thou ponder
Eight souls in Noah's ark were living yonder.

Sometimes the watchman's rhymes didn't make much sense to her, but Kate liked to hear them anyway. They were comforting, especially on a night like this with the danger so near.

She wondered about the men and boys in the town who were keeping watch. She thought about Peter, who would be one of them. Without a stone building to protect him, she hoped that he would be safe through the night.

She clutched her mother's Bible closer to her for comfort, and the words of the Psalm Uncle Josh had told her to remember, whenever she was lonely or frightened, slipped into her mind. She said the words to herself. She said them for Peter, too.

"The Lord is my light and salvation; whom shall I fear? The Lord is the strength of my life; of whom shall I be afraid?"

With these comforting thoughts she closed her eyes. She was about to try to get some sleep when a soft whimpering sounded near her bed.

Kate sat up and looked around her. The whimpering cry seemed to be coming from the row of beds in front of her. She leaned over the side of her own bed and whispered, "Johanna!"

There was no answer. Could Johanna be asleep already?

"Johanna! Wake up!" she whispered again.

But Johanna gave a little groan and rolled over on

her other side. If her friend could sleep so soundly on a night like this, it would be wrong to wake her, Kate thought. Anyway, the child was probably just having a bad dream and would soon quiet down.

But the whimpering kept on, a sad, soft sobbing, and Kate knew that the child was awake. She looked at Sister Magdalena, who was keeping watch by the door. The woman had her eyes closed and her head bent, but she was not asleep. Between the child's soft sobs Kate could hear her praying.

Kate slipped from her cot to the one in front of hers. She bent over the whimpering child. "Shhh. It will be all right," she murmured.

The child stopped sobbing and looked up at her. Although in the dim light she could not see him distinctly, she knew at once who he was. The face staring up at her was dark and solemn; the hair was long and black; the eyes were big and brown.

A tightness gathered inside her as she stared back at the Indian boy. How strange his dark face seemed in the shadows! There was something about it—a sorrow so deep that she felt it, too.

It was then that the full meaning of Sister Magdalena's words came to her, and she knew that the Indian boy must be crying for his parents as she so often at night had cried for hers. Nathan's parents, like her own, were victims of this terrible war. Only it was English soldiers who had killed his parents when they raided and burned his village. *Why do people have to be so cruel to one another?* she cried in silence. It wasn't just the Indians who raided settlements; it was white men, too.

With a trembling hand she reached out to touch the

Indian boy. Her fingers felt his warm face, his cheeks moist with tears. She did not know whether he could understand her or not, but she whispered in a comforting voice, "I know how you feel, Nathan. I have lost my parents, too."

Then she did something she thought she could never do. She lay down on the narrow bed beside the little boy and held him close in her arms. His stiff body relaxed a little. Strange that this Indian boy should remind her of her own seven-year-old brother. She remembered how she used to slip into Benjamin's bed in the cabin loft to console him when he had a stomachache or a bad dream. Oh, how she hoped that in some Indian wigwam gentle arms were reaching out for her brother, too.

Nathan accepted her comfort and snuggled up close to her. She glanced down at the child, who had stopped crying and whose eyelids were flickering shut with sleep. At that moment a strange happiness surged through her, a happiness she had never known before.

Gone were the sorrow, the anger, and the bitter hatred. Nathan needed her, and she needed him. An Indian could be her friend, her brother.

14

Keeping the Watch

Peter shivered as he stood behind the log stockade and kept watch. Even though he wore his thick woolen blanket coat and the blue muffler Johanna had knit for him, the cold night wind bit through his lean body and stung his cheeks.

Joseph Sturgis stood by his side. The two boys had become close friends and were inseparable these days. They had volunteered to take their turns together, keeping the watch the second half of the night.

"Abide watchful at your posts," Brother Joseph had instructed them. "Young eyes are sharper than old ones. If you see signs of French Indians, alert the other watchmen immediately. We must be forever vigilant, for we have the care of over four hundred souls in our keeping."

Neither Peter nor Joseph had a musket; their sharp eyes were their only weapons. Even though the regular watchmen were armed, they were instructed to use their muskets only to signal to one another if they saw marauding Indians. Hopefully the red men, hearing the shots, would realize that the town was well guarded and would be frightened away. The Brethren did not want to harm even enemy Indians, and Peter had prayed there would be no bloodshed.

The night was clear and cold. The moon hung like a bright lantern in the sky. Its light cast long blue shadows of buildings and trees across the snowy ground.

On a night like this Peter could see how easy it would be for a band of raiding Indians to make their way through the dark forest surrounding the town. On such a night they would not need a firebrand to light their way. They could slip from behind trees and bushes, unseen, and be upon the town before anyone knew it. His eyes burned from staring so hard at the woods across the creek, but he scarcely blinked for fear that he might miss a movement behind a dark tree or a bush.

Now and then the boys talked in hushed tones to keep themselves alert. In the other watchtowers that guarded the approaches to town other men and boys stood watching and talking, too. They were too cold and frightened to feel sleepy; even so, the second half of the night stretched out long before them.

They welcomed the sound of the bell in the Bell Tower that struck the quarter hours, the half hour, and the hour. And it was comforting to hear the voice of Brother Matthias as he made his rounds.

'Twas two! On Jesus wait this silent season,
Ye too so near related, will and reason.

"Two o'clock," Joseph said in a tight voice. "Four more hours until dawn breaks."

Although Joseph was still recovering from the massacre at Gnadenhuetten, he had volunteered to join in the watch tonight. He wanted to do all he could to help protect his people from another terrible raid.

Now and then the boys glanced back at the stone houses, Joseph thinking of the babies and little children sleeping there and Peter thinking of Kate and Johanna. The heavy silence of the town was broken only by Brother Matthias' boots crunching back and forth over the frozen crust of snow.

The bell on the Bell House rang the hour again, and the watchman chanted:

The clock in three! The blessed three do merit.
The best of praise from body, soul, and spirit.

Three o'clock—one of the darkest and coldest hours before the dawn. The boys stamped their feet to keep warm. Peter buried his chin into his muffler, his shoulders hunched against the night air. His whole body shook, but now more from fear than from the cold. An anxious thought kept nagging at the back of his mind. Only two more hours until the morning bell rang. Surely the Indians would attack by then. No matter how cold and tired he and Joseph were, they must be more watchful now than ever.

Suddenly Joseph stopped stamping his feet and stood dead still. His sharp eyes had spotted something. He nudged Peter and pointed.

Against the white snow the boys glimpsed a moving shadow. A dark shape was running, haunched over like an animal, through the trees on the other side of the creek. Joseph sucked in his breath. "Only an Indian runs like that!"

No sooner had he spoken than a shot rang out across the creek. Both boys jumped. Peter felt his whole body trembling. The attack! It was beginning!

Now the watchmen began to fire their muskets from the watchtowers to warn the enemy. Men ran from the Brethren's House, their heavy boots pounding over the frozen snow. They joined the watchmen behind the stockade. There they waited in breathless silence, the Bishop among them. From where he stood, Peter could see Brother Joseph's head bent in silent prayer, the only weapon against the attack that he would allow himself.

Suddenly all was quiet again. The woods across the creek stood still and bare, as if no Indian had been running through the trees or no shot had been fired. Peter rubbed his eyes. Had he and Joseph just imagined that they saw the crouched form of an Indian in the dark woods? It could have been a deer or a wolf. Yet the gunshot had been real enough. The other watchmen had heard it, too.

The men and boys behind the stockade waited and watched. A silence, more ominous than before, hung over the town. Even Brother Matthias had paused on his rounds and stood silently waiting.

Peter stole an anxious glance around him. The sturdy stone houses, the stockade, and everything in the town seemed altered somehow—fragile and unfamiliar—as if their strength that he had depended upon

The crouching shapes prepared to rush along the bottomland for the hill.

could collapse and go up in flames at any moment.

All at once he felt very much like a frightened little boy and wanted to cry. He bit his lip and hoped he would not panic and run. He was a man now, and he had been sent here to help keep the watch. No longer could he hide behind the thick walls of the stone house like a child. Tightening his hands into fists, he looked into the dark sky and prayed.

• • •

From the stockade the watchers could not see what was happening in the forest behind the Indian House. They could not see the dark figures, tense and waiting, now crouched along the creek bank by the milldam. The big stone mill hid the shadowy forms from view.

The hour neared four. Soon the first crack of daylight would be breaking through high feathers of clouds on the eastern horizon. Somewhere among the farm buildings on the hill an early cock crowed. The dark forms began to creep across the ice on the dam. At the mill they crouched low so that they would not be seen by a wakeful refugee housed there.

The bell in the Bell Tower sounded four long tones. To the war party hidden behind the mill, it was the signal to attack. The crouching shapes prepared to rush across the bottomland for the hill. In a moment they would give their terrible war whoops. With muskets, tomahawks, and firebrands they would attack the town. Their bodies as tense as whipcord, they waited for their leader to give the final signal.

As they waited for that moment, the quiet darkness was suddenly filled, not with their leader's war whoop, but with a strange, unearthly sound—a sound the French Indians from the Wyoming Valley had never heard before. It rose on the night air, surging wild and exultant above the stone houses. It seemed to be coming from the sky.

The Indians stopped in their tracks and listened with awe. Their leader lowered his tomahawk and looked around him. But all he glimpsed was the dark form of the tall Indian scout, called Running Deer, moving swiftly across the milldam. The Indian joined the band of raiders at the mill.

"What is it?" they asked with frightened voices as the haunting tones swirled above them.

The tall Indian flung back his head and looked up at

the sky. "It is the voice of the white man's Great Spirit," he said in deep, reverent tones.

"What does the Great Spirit say?" asked their leader.

"The Great Spirit is protecting his people and warns you not to harm the settlement."

The tall Indian turned and fled back across the dam and into the forest. The strange voice of the white man's God continued. It was more frightening to the raiding party than the gunshots from the stockade. Fearfully they turned and followed the tall Indian back into the forest until the dark trees enveloped them all.

•   •   •

From the stockade Peter and Joseph looked up at the platform on top of the Brethren's House. In the dim moonlight they could hardly make out the shadowy forms of the men standing there. With hearts full of joy they listened as the trombone choir heralded the coming of Christmas Day.

"It will soon be dawn and the Indians have not attacked!" Joseph said with awe.

"The danger is over!" exclaimed Peter.

"Don't speak too soon," a watchman chided. "We'll keep our posts until day breaks."

Everyone behind the stockade stayed alert. At five the rising bell rang out, and later Brother Matthias joyfully chanted,

> The clock is six and I go off my station
> Now Brethren, watch yourselves for your salvation.

Then as the pearly gray in the east grew bright, so did their hopes. At last the first rays of the sun touched the wooded hills across the river. In the awakening sky hung the morning star. It shone brightly over the stone buildings and the wooden stockade. It shone above the now-empty forest across the creek.

The people in Bethlehem were replenishing their fires. Spirals of smoke curled from the chimneys. Christmas Day was beginning.

Weary but happy, Peter and Joseph looked at each other. Heads thrown back, they laughed into the brightening day. Then arm in arm, they left the stockade.

15

The Christmas
Surprise

In the dormitory of the Family House, Kate awoke
with a start. She wondered what the sound was that
had awakened her so suddenly. A shiver of alarm ran
through her. Had the Indians attacked?

But as she became fully awake and listened to the
exultant notes soar through the cold, crisp air, her fear
left and her heart surged with happiness. Trombones!
It was the trombone choir on the Brethren's rooftop
that she heard, playing the Christmas chorales just as
Brother Joseph had said they would.

The sound of the trombones caused Sister Magdalena
to stir on her chair by the doorway. She lifted her
weary head. In the lamplight her face looked strained
from her all-night vigil, but the stern lips broke into a
happy prayer of thanksgiving. It was Christmas morn-

ing and they were alive and safe. The danger was over.

The children, awakened by the trombones, slipped out of their beds and ran to the dormer windows. Rubbing away the frost on the panes, they peered out at the dark figures standing behind the balustrade on the Brethren's roof. As soon as she was dressed, Kate joined them, and as she listened to the stirring notes of the old Christmas chorales, she wondered if Peter was hearing them, too.

She was so preoccupied with her happy thoughts that she was barely aware of the small, rough hand seeking hers. From the light of her candle she looked down at the somber face and startled dark eyes of the Indian boy. The sound of the trombones that was making her feel so happy was frightening him.

She drew him to the window and pointed to the roof of the Brethren's House. "It is the trombone choir playing the Christmas chorales, Nathan." Then she pointed to the bright star shining in the sky. "See the morning star? It is the star the children sing about. It shines over Bethlehem this Christmas morning." She gave a happy little laugh. "There is nothing to fear now."

Even though the boy did not understand her words, he seemed to understand what he had meant. He looked at the men with their strange horns on the roof of the Brethren's House. Then he gazed up at the morning star. The look of fear left his face and wonder filled his eyes.

Remembering what day this was, the children soon forgot about the trombones. They left the windows and grabbed their clothes from the row of wooden pegs that lined the room. There followed a scramble to get dressed. Kate helped Johanna and the Sisters dress the babies and smaller children. When the morning bell rang, they were ready and their beds were made.

Kate hurried across the room to see about Nathan. He had dressed himself, but the noise and exuberance of the children confused him. He took her hand and held it tightly as they got into line with the others. When they passed through the doorway, Sister Magdalena nodded her head with approval, and a rare smile came to her lips when she saw Kate holding the Indian boy's hand.

After breakfast, which the children gobbled down as fast as they could, the Sisters led them to the Christmas room. The warden fitted her key into the lock, and the door swung open to the wondrous sight of the Christmas surprise.

A hush settled over the noisy children as they entered the candlelit room. With ahs and ohs they walked up to the Christmas crib to admire the nativity scene. There was the Wonder Child in his manger of straw with the carved figures of Mary and Joseph standing beside it. Moss-covered rocks formed the hills above the stable, where shepherds watched their large flocks of sheep.

Kate picked up one of the woolly sheep with its stiff wooden legs and vermilion nose and handed it to Nathan. The little boy's eyes lighted up as he admired his gift. Kate hoped that the sheep she gave him was one that she had helped to make.

Beyond the shepherds and their flocks were carved figures of the three wise men in their colorful robes. Across a desert of yellow sawdust they were following the star that glittered above the little stable. Around the entire scene were several pyramids of evergreen

*There was the Wonder Child in his manger of straw
with the carved figures of Mary and Joseph.*

boughs, shaped like little trees and decorated with
small brown candles. From the branches of the largest
pyramid hung polished apples and the verses the girls
had printed.

Kate was as thrilled as the children. She had never
seen a Christmas crib before, and this one was truly
more wonderful than she had ever imagined.

"Didn't I tell you how wonderful it would be?"
Johanna exclaimed, bubbling over with enthusiasm as
she slipped alongside Kate and Nathan.

"It's just like Christmas in the old country," murmured a Sister who stood near them. "As long as I
remember, we always had a *Krippe* for our Christmas
surprise."

All the children now crowded around the crib, pointing out the wonders to one another eagerly.

"Baby Jesus is smiling."

"And so are Mary and Joseph."

"Look at the cow and donkey in the stable. Are they smiling, too?"

"I like the sheep best. Look how woolly they are."

While all this was going on, the warden by the door was watching anxiously, as if she was expecting someone. When she heard the outside door open, her face brightened. She hurried down the hall to join the man who was making his way to the Christmas room. With him was a group of refugee children. They all crowded into the room together.

"Brother Joseph!" the Moravian children called as soon as they spied their Bishop. "Come, see our Christmas surprise!"

The Bishop walked up to the crib. The children crowded around him and pointed out each wonder. He smiled and put his arms around as many of them as he could. He is a father to them all this Christmas day, Kate thought, smiling to herself.

"It is a wonderful *Krippe*," the Bishop said. "Would you like to hear the Christmas story that this crib reminds us of?"

"Yes! Yes!" chorused the children.

Lifting a small refugee child so that she could see over the heads of the others, Brother Joseph began: " 'And Mary brought forth her firstborn son, and wrapped him in swaddling clothes, and laid him in a manger; because there was no room for them in the inn. And there were in the same country shepherds abiding in the field, keeping watch over their flock by night. . . . ' "

After the story of the first Christmas was told, the Moravian children shared their Christmas love feast with the refugee children. Sugar buns were passed around with mugs of peppermint tea. Then each child was given a woolly sheep, an apple, and one of the colorful verses that hung on the evergreen boughs.

Carols were sung while the warden handed out little brown beeswax candles. Everyone had a candle, even the babies. Brother Joseph lighted his candle from the one that shone above the little stable. From his candle Sister Magdalena lighted hers. She held her candle to the child next to her and the child passed on the light to his neighbor. The girls and Sisters held lighted candles for the younger children and the babies. As Kate touched her candle to Nathan's, she smiled down at him. For the first time the Indian boy smiled back.

When all the candles were lighted, the Moravian children sang their Christmas hymn for the Bishop.

> Morning Star, O cheering sight!
> Ere Thou cam'st how dark earth's night.

Tears of happiness welled up in Kate's eyes as she sang. How grateful she was that the morning star shone over a happy Bethlehem this Christmas day!

• • •

When Peter came to fill the woodbox the next morning, Kate and Johanna told him all about the Christmas crib and how much the children loved it.

"Sister Esther was right," Johanna said. "It was the best Christmas surprise ever."

"Then it was well worth the risk of going into the

woods for the greens," Peter said, a smile curving his lips.

He, in turn, told them about the Christmas Eve watch and how surprised they all were that the Indians did not attack.

"Maybe it was because they knew the town was well guarded," Johanna suggested.

Peter nodded thoughtfully, "It could be. David Zeisberger thinks that the Indian we saw across the creek was Brother Aaron setting out before dawn for the Wyoming Valley. Brother David said that Brother Aaron will be spending the winter at Wyoming to give comfort to our Christian Indians there."

Peter paused with a puzzled frown. "Of course, we did hear the gunshot across the creek, but maybe one of the Indians at the Indian House thought he had heard an animal or something outside."

"Well, let's not think anymore about it," Kate said with an inward sigh of relief. "Let's just be thankful that the Indians didn't attack and let's hope they never will."

After a joyful Christmas season, the long gray days of winter passed uneventfully with no further threats of an Indian attack. Now that Mr. Franklin and the commissioners had a line of forts built along the Blue Mountain, where settlers could gather for protection in case of danger, many refugees were returning to their settlements to rebuild their burned houses.

In the early spring when the mountain trails were clear of drifted snow, Brother Aaron returned to Bethlehem from the Wyoming Valley. He had a strange story to tell.

He told how, just before dawn on Christmas morning

as he was starting out for the Wyoming Valley, he had met a band of Delawares and Shawnees. They were painted for war and were coming down the wooded hill in back of the Indian House when he first saw them. The leader shot his musket into the air as a signal for Brother Aaron to identify himself. It was that musket shot that the watchers at the stockade had heard.

The Indian scout went on to tell how he had followed the band across the frozen milldam, and when they heard the trombones how he had persuaded them to flee, telling them that it was the white man's Great Spirit speaking, warning them not to attack. He led them back across the creek and into the dark forest. They did not suspect that Brother Aaron was a Moravian Indian. To them he was Running Deer, the Indian scout who carried messages between the Wyoming Valley and the white man's villages.

"So now we know why the Indians did not attack," Johanna exclaimed when the girls heard Brother Aaron's story from the Sisters. "It was the trombone choir and Brother Aaron who saved Bethlehem on Christmas morning!"

Sister Magdalena gave her a meaningful look. "And, of course, God's mercy," she reminded them all. "We must not forget that!"

One day when Peter came to the Sisters' House to fill the woodbox, he was whistling a happy tune. "I talked to Brother Joseph yesterday about becoming a missionary, and he has encouraged me," Peter told them, his face beaming. "And David Zeisberger said he would teach me the Indian dialects."

"Oh, that's wonderful, Peter," Kate said. "You have always wanted to be a missionary like David Zeisberger." She paused thoughtfully, then added, "I wish that I, too, could learn the Indian dialects."

Johanna swung around and looked at her friend with surprise. "*You* want to learn the Indian language, Kate?" she exclaimed.

Kate nodded. "I was thinking of Nathan and how, so often, I wished that I could talk with him in his own language."

Peter's blue eyes regarded her warmly. "I'll ask Brother David if I can share my lessons with you, Kate," he offered.

"You will?" she asked, returning the smile in his eyes. "Oh, Peter, that would be wonderful!"

Her heart throbbed with happiness. It was good to have Peter and Johanna and Nathan for friends. And it was a good feeling not to hate any more but to love everyone in her world.

16

Kate's Decision

The wild locust trees in the Bell House Square were covered with white blossoms and by the creek the willows were misty green when Uncle Josh returned to Bethlehem.

Kate was at the creek on that bright day, gathering watercress with Johanna, Anna Catherine, and Regina. All four girls looked up curiously when they heard the sharp drumming of hoofbeats on the log bridge. Johanna gave the horseman a fleeting glance, then followed Anna Catherine and Regina along the creek to continue their gathering. But Kate kept staring at the horseman, shading her eyes so that she could see him better. There was something familiar about this buckskin-clad rider and his big horse. When he shifted his weight in the saddle and lifted his head, she knew.

Dropping her basket of watercress, she ran to the bridge, stumbling over tangled roots along the creek bank in her hurry. "Uncle Josh!" she shouted.

The circuit rider reined in his mount, and with one easy motion he swung down from the saddle and gathered his niece in his arms.

"Uncle Josh, you've come back!"

"Of course I've come back, Kate," Joshua Stewart told her, laughing. "Didn't I promise I would?" He looked a long time at his niece. "It's good to see you again, Katie. Oh, how good it is!"

"I know, Uncle Josh. It's good to see you again, too." She flung her arms around his neck and gave him a happy squeeze. "I am so glad you kept safe through this winter."

For a long moment they clung to each other, then Kate drew back and looked up at her uncle with anxious eyes. "Have you any news about Benjamin?"

The happy expression melted from her uncle's face and he shook his head. "I have asked every Indian trader I met on my journeys through the back country about the boy, but no one has seen or heard of him. They told me that the Delawares and Shawnees keep their captives well hidden in their lodges when strangers come to their villages, so that no one can see them."

Kate nodded sadly. "That's what David Zeisberger told me. He has asked his Indian friends to keep a lookout for Benjamin, but they have not seen him either. Brother David thinks Benjamin may have been taken to an Indian village far away from Wyoming."

"It is possible," Uncle Josh said.

He took her hand in his big one and looked down as if he were studying it. "We will not stop searching for

Benjamin. Meanwhile, we will pray that he is safe and learns to live contentedly with his captors. I do know this, that the Delawares and Shawnees are fond of children and treat captive ones as their own."

As she listened to Uncle Josh, thoughts of Nathan flashed through her mind. She thought about how the Indian boy was adjusting to the love and care of his strange new home. No longer did he cry for his village or his parents, and perhaps no longer did Benjamin.

Leading the big bay by the lead line, Joshua Stewart walked with his niece across the bottomland and up the hill.

As they walked along, he said, "Since Benjamin Franklin has seen to it that forts are built along the Blue Mountain, the back country has again become a safe place to live. I found a pleasant settlement on the south side of the mountain where settlers have built new cabins. A mill to attract farmers is located by a good stream, and the settlers are now at work building a log church. They have asked me to be their preacher."

He paused, beaming down at his niece. "But, Kate, I have almost forgotten the most important news of all," he went on, his eyes twinkling. "At the settlement I met a bonnie lass. Her name is Amanda, and I have asked her to be my wife. We will be wed this summer as soon as I finish building our cabin. Then I will have a home for both of you."

"Oh, Uncle Josh, that's the best news ever!" Kate exclaimed with delight.

Her uncle smiled down at her. "Amanda's parents have offered to take us in until our cabin is finished. I know you'll like them, Kate. It will be so good to have my family with me again."

When they reached the top of the hill, he said, "I'll see the Bishop and thank him for keeping you safe this winter. Then tomorrow we'll leave for the back country."

• • •

That night Kate packed her mother's Bible and the clothes the Sisters had given her in a bundle that would fit into Uncle Josh's saddlebag. Joseph Sturgis' moccasins she kept out to wear on the trail the next day.

I'm going home with Uncle Josh! I'm going home to the back country! The words pulsed in her head as she folded her clothes. She had looked forward to this day all through the long winter, and now that it had come she should be overjoyed. And she was happy about the cabin Uncle Josh was building. But strangely, she realized, it was for Uncle Josh and Amanda, and not so much for herself, that she felt so blissful.

Johanna was not her usual jolly self as she watched Kate pack. "I shall miss you, Kate," she said, trying hard to keep her lips from trembling.

Kate sat down beside her friend and felt a tug of sadness at her own heart.

"Oh, Johanna, I shall miss you, too," she replied.

Later that night Kate turned restlessly on her feather tick. Was she sleepless because she was so excited about Uncle Josh's return and the new home she was going to? Or was it the memory of Johanna's trembling lips and Peter's brave smile and sad blue eyes when he heard that her uncle had come for her, that kept her awake?

She let out a deep sigh and blinked up at the high

arched ceiling of the dormitory. No longer did this big stone building seem like a prison to her. Now it symbolized the sturdy, steadfast love of those who occupied it.

Bethlehem—so much had happened to her here. No longer was she the same angry, frightened girl who had ridden up the hill and into town that October day with her uncle. Nor was she the same girl who had once lived at Penn's Creek. The little cabin in the clearing, her parents, and her brother were gone—and so was that carefree girl who had lived there with them.

She forced her thoughts back to the present. She must not forget to say good-bye to Nathan. He had learned to love and to trust her. She must explain very carefully why she was leaving.

As soon as breakfast was over the next morning, Kate walked down the lane that led to the Family House. The Indian boy was in the yard, playing with the other children. They were all laughing and shouting, happy to be outside again in the warm spring sunshine.

When he saw her, Nathan ran to meet her, calling her name. But when he saw the sad look in her eyes, his brown face sobered.

Now that she was here, standing before Nathan, Kate wondered how she could ever tell him that she was leaving, maybe never to see him again.

She was trying to find courage to say good-bye when a hand touched her shoulder. Uncle Josh had seen her walking down the lane from the Brethren's House, where he had spent the night, and had come looking for her.

"Are you ready, Kate?" he asked. "We'd best be going, for we have a long journey ahead of us."

She hesitated, and a salty tear slid down her cheek. With the back of her hand she brushed it away, but the thoughts that had been churning around in her mind now spilled out in a gush of words.

"Oh, Uncle Josh, I can't go back with you!" she burst out, as surprised as he was at her words. She placed her hand on his arm and tried to explain. "You will have Amanda to look after you, Uncle Josh, and to be your family. And—and Nathan needs me here."

Even to her own ears her protest sounded rather lame and she thought Uncle Josh would think so, too, and brush it aside.

But he didn't. Instead, he looked at the Indian boy, then turned and looked deeply into her eyes. "Are you sure you want to stay, Kate?"

She nodded and fumbled for Nathan's hand. "I am sure, Uncle Josh. Brother Joseph said that the Indians who are our friends need our help now more than ever."

Joshua Stewart was silent for a moment. Then he said, "I shall miss you, Kate." He frowned thoughtfully. "What will the Bishop have to say about your decision to stay?"

"I don't know," answered Kate in a small voice. "I guess I'll have to ask him."

She gave Nathan's hand a little squeeze and forced a smile on her lips. Reassured by her smile, the Indian boy ran to join his playmates.

Kate and her uncle walked up the lane in silence. When they turned in at the Community House, Uncle Josh paused by the door and took her hand in his. "As I said before, I shall miss you, Kate. But now I know that you have changed from a girl to a woman and can make your own decisions. I am proud of you for that."

Kate drew in a quick breath. "Then you don't mind if I stay in Bethlehem?" she asked.

He took her arm in his and smiled down at her. "You may stay, Katie, as far as I'm concerned. Come, let's ask the Bishop."

When Brother Joseph had heard about Kate's decision to stay in Bethlehem, he was more pleased than surprised.

"You have learned much since that day before Christmas when I found you, a frightened girl, in the Chapel," he said. "You have learned to accept God's will and to be brave. But most of all you have learned to love all God's children and to live in peace with them. Someday, perhaps, with your knowledge of the back country, you might like to enter the mission field."

She looked up with surprise at his words. She had never thought about entering the mission field, but now that Brother Joseph had mentioned it, she knew that was exactly what she wanted to do. She had learned to love Bethlehem, but she loved the back country, too. And maybe someday in a Delaware or Shawnee village she would find Benjamin.

"Oh, thank you, Brother Joseph!" she said. "I would like that."

Her happiness was now complete. The Bishop had given her another reason for staying. A new life was opening up for her here where she was loved and needed. Bethlehem was now her home.

While Uncle Josh and Brother Joseph continued talking, Kate slipped out of the Community House and made her way to the Bell House Square. She couldn't wait a moment longer to tell her friends of her decision.

She found Peter filling the woodbox and Johanna was with him. Forgetting what Sister Magdalena had taught her about being ladylike, Kate raced across the Bell House Square and greeted her two friends breathlessly.

"I'm staying!" she called out as she ran. "I'm not returning with Uncle Josh. I'm staying right here in Bethlehem!"

Johanna and Peter stared at her with surprise.

"Brother Joseph said I could stay," she went on in a rush of words. "And I'm going to continue my study of the Indian dialects so that I can become a missionary like you, Peter."

At Kate's words, Johanna twirled around happily, almost knocking off her *Haube* in her enthusiasm. Peter had stars in his eyes as he ran to meet her.

Kate looked up into his strong, young face, and her own eyes sparkled with happiness at the thought of sharing his future.

The white locust blossoms shone silver against the blue morning sky. The new grass sparkled as green as emerald. On either side of the square the big stone buildings reached out protective arms, drawing the three young people together.

Author's Note

From one generation to another the old story is told
of how, in 1755, the town of Bethlehem, Pennsylvania,
was saved from an Indian attack by a chorus of
trombones heralding the coming of Christmas morning
from the rooftop of the Brethren's House. That was a
most happy Christmas surprise for the Moravian settlers that year. The other surprise, of course, was the
traditional *Krippe*, an annual surprise for the children
on Christmas day.

The year, 1755, during the French and Indian War,
was a terrible time for the settlers in the back country
of Pennsylvania. Many settlements were raided by
French Indians and their population massacred. The
Moravian town of Bethlehem, with its large stone
buildings, became a haven for many refugees of these
raids.

With their sublime faith that only God could protect them, the peaceful Moravians of Bethlehem survived the terrible year. Unlike their neighbors in nearby settlements, they did not look upon the Indians as their enemies but regarded every red man as a brother. Their missionary work among the Indians, with its dangers and privations, was a glowing example of their brotherly love.

The background and historical events in this book are as accurate as my research could make them. Many of the old original Moravian buildings, such as the Brethren's House and those in the Bell House Square, can be seen today in Bethlehem, just as they had stood in 1755. At Christmastime the children of Bethlehem still look forward to the *Krippe,* now called the community *Putz,* and still listen to the trombone chorales. And every year they sing their favorite Christmas hymn, "Morning Star," at the Christmas vesper service.

The music of this old hymn was originally written by J. A. Freylinghausen in 1704. This was the tune which the Moravian children sang in 1755. In 1836 the Reverend F. F. Hagen wrote the antiphonal music for the old hymn which is sung at the present time. The words were written by Johann Scheffler in 1657.

Bishop Spangenberg, David Zeisberger, Joseph Sturgis, Dr. Otto, Justice Timothy Horsfield, Brother Popplewell, and Valentine Haidt were real people living in Bethlehem in 1755. Also authentic were the Moravian missionaries at Gnadenhuetten and what had happened to them. The raid at Penn's Creek Settlement on October 16, 1755, was authentic, too.

Although Kate, Johanna, and Peter are imaginary characters, they represent the young people in that period of history who suffered the perils of their time, but by doing so gained tolerance and an abiding faith.

I have taken certain liberties by using Bishop Spangenberg and David Zeisberger in several imaginary scenes to further my plot. However, their words and actions would be within keeping of their personalities in real life.

For most of my historical references I am indebted to *A History of Bethlehem, Pennsylvania, 1741-1892,* by Joseph Mortimer Levering; *Bethlehem of Pennsylvania, the First One Hundred Years,* edited by W. Ross Yates and Committee; *Snow over Bethlehem,* by Katherine Milhous; *The Morning Star,* by Lucille Wallower; *Sketches of Early Bethlehem* and *Lehigh Valley, the Unsuspected,* by Richmond E. Myers; *Moravian Customs,* by Harry E. Stocker; *Customs and Practices of the Moravian Church,* by Adelaide L. Fries; and *A Century of Moravian Sisters,* by Elizabeth Myers.

I want to thank Beth Pearce, Museum consultant-curator of the Moravian Historical Society; Mary Catherine Smith, curator of Historic Bethlehem, Inc.; Margaret Danneberger; and Jeanette Zug for their personal assistance to the many questions I had about Bethlehem of 1755. I also want to thank my husband, Carl L. Moore, a volunteer guide for Historic Bethlehem, Inc., for his help and encouragement in writing this book.

Word List

Apothecary—one who prepares medicine from herbs; a physician in the eighteenth century. Also a physician's office in the eighteenth century, or a place where medicines were dispensed.

Der Platz—the town square.

Gemein Haus—Community House.

Gnadenhuetten—Huts of Grace. A Moravian Indian mission village founded in 1746 at the junction of the Mahoning Creek and the Lehigh River. It is now the town of Lehighton, Pennsylvania.

Haube—the plain white cap worn by all Moravian women and girls.

Krippe—a Christmas crib, or nativity scene, depicting the birth of Christ.

Linsey-woolsey—a coarse cloth of wool and linen.

Love feast—a Christian fellowship of eating and drinking together on special occasions, imitating the agape of the early Christians. Buns and coffee or tea were served.

Moravian—a Christian denomination founded in Moravia and Bohemia (now Czechoslovakia) by the reform movement of John Hus. The early Moravians were known for their pacifist views and their missionary zeal.

Nazareth—a Moravian settlement ten miles north of Bethlehem.

Piggin—a small wooden bucket.

Saxony—now part of East Germany.

Singstunde—a religious service devoted to singing, usually at the end of the day.

Spinet—forerunner of the piano.

Zither—a musical instrument with strings over a shallow soundboard. The strings are plucked with a small piece of ivory.

The Author

Ruth Nulton Moore was born in Easton, Pennsylvania, and now lives in Bethlehem, Pennsylvania, with her husband, Carl, a professor emeritus at Lehigh University. They have two sons, three granddaughters, and two grandsons.

A former schoolteacher, Mrs. Moore has written for children's magazines and is author of seventeen juveniles. *Danger in the Pines* won Christian School's C. S. Lewis Silver Medallion, and *In Search of Liberty* received the Silver Angel Award from Religion in Media. Her books have been translated into Swedish, Finnish, German, and Spanish.

Mrs. Moore is a member of Children's Authors and Illustrators of Philadelphia, and her biography appears in *Contemporary Authors, The International Authors and Writers Who's Who,* and *Pennsylvania Women in History.* When she is not at her typewriter, she is busy lecturing about the art of writing to students in the public schools and colleges in her area.

She belongs to Christ Church, United Church of Christ, where she has been a Sunday school teacher.